The German Spy

Richard G. Hole

The German Spy
A World War II Novel

Richard G. Hole

World War II

SYNOPSIS

He walked over to a closet sticking it to the right wall. A hanging suit and a suitcase appeared before his eyes. He fingered the suit without hearing the rustle of paper he expected. He remembered very well that she had told him that he was carrying an envelope with instructions.

He opened the suitcase, which appeared completely empty.

He gritted his teeth, grunting a curse. He began feeling the suitcase, to no avail. It was very simple and it was not possible to think of a double bottom. Of course, that had to be checked ...

But in those moments, he was paralyzed, almost blinded by the light, much more intense than that of the flashlight, which had suddenly struck the room. Then he heard the door to the room close quietly and a voice said:

"Do not move. I'm targeting you ...

THE GERMAN SPY

1

The Tegeler See, located north-west of Berlin, surrounded by green lawns and forests, looked serene, placid, in the summer of 1942.

The calm and blue waters, calm, almost immobile, also seemed endowed with the particular atmosphere that enveloped the city of Berlin, where everything indicated that the war was being won. The confidence of the people was almost absolute in this regard.

The surface of the lake presented the joyous colors that small sailing boats, pleasure boats, and some sloops that sail lazily lend. The piers, on the shores of the lake, were crowded with small boats with white sail, and with people who interrupted the placid atmosphere with their somewhat timid conversations.

A woman was walking in the direction of one of the sloops tied to the tiny dock.

A woman with long dark brown hair, tall, with a narrow waist and high bust. She was wearing a light pink sweater and a slightly darker skirt; the skirt, although unprovoked, clung to her hips, highlighting soft, firm shapes. His face, somewhat long, thin, with slightly protruding cheekbones, had a strange attractiveness, despite the somewhat hard fold of the woman's pink lips. A pair of blue eyes, intelligent, a little cold, distant, added to Gretel Hagen's personality.

Gretel casually climbed the light white ladders on the sloop, and stepped onto the deck of the boat. She raised the ladder on board herself. Then he looked at the man who was leaning back against the mast of the light craft.

The man smiled.

"Shall we take a walk, Gretel?"

"It will be for the best, right?" The woman murmured.

"Naturally. It will be dark soon, and the Tegeler never lends itself better to confidences ... of whatever kind.

"I understand" smiled Gretel.

When Gretel smiled, her cheekbones rose slightly and her blue pupils lost their coolness, it also seemed that she was getting closer to her interlocutor.

The man strode aft, holding the rod. He sat down on a stool close to the deck, and signaled to Gretel, as the sloop, its sails taut in the breeze, was unmooring.

Everything was natural there. Anyone who had paid attention to this strange couple would have shrugged. We say the strange couple because that man was at least twice Gretel's age. Even that was common in Nazi Germany.

Gretel sat next to the man, silently. She let the breeze ruffle her hair slightly, and took a deep breath. That walk by the lake would be, after all, a sedative; a little escape from the stress she had endured for about six months. It would be an escape as long as this man, Horst Anthelme, didn't say otherwise.

Finally, serenely, Gretel looked at the man and said:

"It must be something important, Horst.

The man smiled.

"And dangerous," he said. I've been studying your file and I have the man we need.

"Where is it?" Asked Gretel.

"In Stockholm.

Gretel arched an eyebrow, looking at Anthelme.

"Stockholm? What is one of our best men doing in Stockholm? Sweden is neutral "he said." Well ... I guess it must be one of the best, since you've noticed him.

"It is, indeed," said Anthelme. An angry anti-Nazi, Gretel. And not only for that reason I have selected him; other factors have played a role. For example, it is precisely in Stockholm. I want to clarify "he smiled" what would have chosen him even if he was in Africa, do you understand?

"You have full confidence in him," Gretel murmured. Who is it?

"His name is Max Kropelin.

Gretel shook her head.

"I don't know him personally," he said.

"No? Well, you will meet him very soon.

Gretel tensed slightly. He looked at this man, in his fifties, almost bald, with myopic glasses, of slight build, but who nevertheless gave a feeling of integrity, of a certain mysterious strength.

"Do you mean that I must leave for Stockholm?" Inquired the young woman.

"You have understood perfectly," Anthelme said firmly.

Gretel sighed.

"When?" He inquired,

"Could it be tonight?

"I think so.

"Do you think?" Anthelme inquired, not looking at the woman.

"Okay, it will be tonight.

Anthelme nodded.

"The route will be Rostock-Copenhagen-Stockholm," he said. You will go alone. You will not be in contact with anyone except, of course, Max Kropelin. I'm sorry to have to mobilize you, but I cannot allow the Gestapo to destroy our organization by a misstep. Now we're starting to get strong, Gretel. The information that we must pass on to Max Kropelin has come to me from our anti-Nazi group in Paris, which means that we will soon be a danger to Nazism. Besides, of course, we must also fight against the enemies of Germany. So we are fighting on two fronts.

"I know all this, Horst," said the girl. What is it about this time?

Anthelme smiled again, the lenses of his glasses flashing.

"Pay attention, Gretel. I suppose you understand the danger of walking around with documents. Therefore, you must entrust all my instructions to your memory "said Anthelme.

"I know," Gretel murmured.

Anthelme lit a cigarette, with a steady hand, leaving the tiller of the sloop in the hands of Gretel, which was already almost in the center of the lake, when the first lights shone in Berlin, like strange eyes, nyctalopes.

A number of sloops circulated around the lake, some of which headed toward the western shore to enjoy the cool Tegelort forest.

After smoking for a few moments in silence, Horst Anthelme began to speak, without being interrupted by Gretel more than a couple of times. Fifteen minutes later, the woman was repeating word for word. The instructions from Anthelme, who, smiling slightly, nodded.

"Perfect," he said, then.

"But there is one point to be clarified," said Gretel. " Should I go clandestinely?

"Yes. Keep in mind that, if you requested to leave the country, you would be fully on the Gestapo list. They would provide you with your passport with the intention of subjecting you to surveillance.

"It's true. Actually, the legal way out is as dangerous as the clandestine one. I prefer the latter, "said Gretel.

"Remember that the biggest risk for you will be in Copenhagen. It is there where you will have to display all your cunning. We know perfectly well that the Gestapo is much more jealous in the occupied countries.

"Don't worry about me, Horst," Gretel replied.

Without further ado, he left the bench he was occupying next to Anthelme, and headed forward. Shortly after, she was in a black bathing suit, which fitted perfectly to the parts that the bathing suit should hide, and revealing the soft white skin of other parts of the body.

There was a slight splash and the girl sank into the waters of the lake, while Anthelme, smiling, steered the wheel in circles so that the breeze would not blow the sloop away.

He saw Gretel reappear and understood what the young woman wanted with that effort of swimming: to temper her nerves, to calm her brain. It was even possible that Gretel was thinking that she would never be able to bathe in that lake again.

* * *

That man, sitting on a nightstand facing the sea, was smoking nervously. Over and over, his brain registered the words written on a small note, which someone had slipped into his pocket the night before.

That someone could only be that woman, with whom he had crossed a few words in Swedish.

Max Kropelin remembered everything perfectly. After a chance meeting on the part of that woman, they drank a drink together. An enigmatic, beautiful woman whose temperament, Max guessed, was very different from that of faded Swedes, which he loved, since a man only gets bored at certain times.

However, this woman proved, at the last moment, that Max had been wrong: she left him little less than planted, although, yes, smiling. And women who smile at dangerous times tend to have a firm character.

Max Kropelin had seen her leave the nightstand, sighing. Another night alone.

Later, in his rented apartment in front of the Stockholm shipyards, he found the note. The first important thing that stood out to Max's eye was that it was written in German: "Ich komme einen morgen wieder." However, the woman was talking in Swedish.

Max had been mulling over the matter and felt uneasy when he realized that this woman had discovered his true nationality. And probably many other things. Anyway, the idea that the beauty was only trying a date more or less destined to the preparation of intimacy, which by the way must be very pleasant, had already been rejected by Max.

For this reason, that German of ordinary stature, but strong, with broad shoulders and a Teutonic head, waited with a certain impatience. The beauty could be a trap.

Even with such deep-seated thought, Max could not help a start, when he finally discovered Gretel Hagen, walking unhurriedly, upright, in the direction of Max's table at the nightstand.

Max, smiling to hide his mistrust, stood up, saluting with a proper nod.

"Sit down," he said, then.

Gretel obeyed, taking a seat across from Max.

"My note will have caused you some annoyance" said Gretel directly, staring at him.

"Why should he bother me?" Max smiled. On the contrary, this quote ...

"Stop fooling around, Max Kropelin" cut the woman, lowering her voice and smiling, as if she had told Max some tenderness.

Max didn't flinch.

"You also know my name," he said. Anything else?

"Countless things" Gretel smiled again, though her eyes remained somewhat cold, fixed on the man's.

"Why wasn't it discovered last night?" Asked Max.

"Simple precaution. I wanted to know if anyone had been curious about me, Kropelin "said Gretel". And I wanted to find out what effect the note was causing. All day I have been walking around Stockholm without noticing that they follow me. That reassures me, you understand?

"Of course. Anyway, I'd rather we talk somewhere safer ... assuming you have something to say to me.

"What do you think I have summoned you for?" Asked Gretel dryly.

"Good ..." Max smiled, slightly. Agree. And it is true that the note has caused me some headaches, since it assumed that you had discovered my identity. I came to fear a trap.

"Not anymore?" Inquired, with some irony, Gretel.

"Why? Now we are together, right?

Gretel blinked. He remembered what Horst Anthelme had told him about the man, well prepared for any contingency. Besides, Max wasn't one to flinch. Only a steely sparkle in his blue-gray pupils showed that nothing would catch him off guard.

"Shall we go to that safer place?" Asked Gretel, in response.

"Agree. It will be at my house.

Gretel pursed her lips, very thin.

"Maybe someone ..." he began to protest, weakly.

"Don't worry" Max smiled mockingly. It is not the first time that a woman enters my house at night. No one will take it into account. Or maybe you are afraid?

"You don't need to be cynical, Kropelin," said Gretel. " Otherwise, I am not afraid. It is not the first time that I have entered a man's house at night.

"Very well. We'll change the subject, "growled Max, a little discounted by Gretel's response." Let's go?

He left a handful of crowns on the table as payment for his drink. He got up, standing next to Gretel. They both started down Ostergotland Avenue, wide, whose headlights provided patches of light to the gardens, through which many couples strolled.

Two minutes later, Max and Gretel mingled with those couples.

2

In his shirt sleeves, Max Kropelin, by the window of that room, which overlooked the shipyards, gazed at the distant reddish lights that made the waters of the Baltic glow, corresponding to so many fishing barges.

To the left, you could see part of Lake Malar, and some of the tiny islands and peninsulas on which Stockholm sits, called by some the Venice of the North.

Max Kropelin turned to Gretel, who was sitting on a sofa, and lit a cigarette.

"Horst Anthelme sent it, all right," Max said, puffing out a puff of smoke. Why you?

"Certain things can be solved better by a woman than a man," said Gretel. " For example, the trip from Copenhagen to Malmö, in those steamers of the line, I did it in a man's cabin. I convinced him that he was running away from the Danish police, because if I named him the Gestapo he might have given up on being nice, After all, I knew how to keep him at bay,

Max smiled crookedly. He sat down next to Gretel.

"Now get started," he said.

“One of our agents in Paris managed to discover a Soviet spy from the 'Gilbert Group', an offshoot of the 'Rote Kapella'. We all know that the Soviets in Paris are dedicated to communicating movements of our troops from West to East of Europe. However, there was an exchange of information, which was the reason that our agent discovered something important: there is a network dedicated to sabotage in Stockholm.

Max frowned.

"What kind of sabotage?" he inquired.

"I thought you would have discovered something," Gretel said.

"Well, he was wrong," growled Max. I'm just a deserter from the army; a man the Gestapo is looking for; and, most especially, an

13

anti-Nazi. It is true that I have carried out some missions, but they were very well exposed to me by the informants. Normally, I am dedicated only to controlling the growing group of anti-Nazis in Stockholm, in the hope that one day we will be strong enough to bring down Hitler. That is, plain and simple, what I hope,

Gretel bit her lower lip.

"Okay," he said. I will continue, You know that Germany buys Swedish steel; an essential war material,

"I know that" Max replied.

"Several of the ships have not reached Germany," Gretel said. That has been hidden by the Gestapo, fearing a loss of prestige among the party.

"Yeah ..." - Max muttered.

"Even some of those ships have jumped here, in the port of Stockholm," continued Gretel. " It is a question, then, of dismantling that Soviet network. The steel must reach Germany; we need it to continue the war. A war that may be won by Germany, but never by the NSD A P. If we lose it, with a more humane internal regime we will be able to soften the tension with the allies.

Max nodded.

"It's clear," he said. What else do we know about that network?

"A man named Pavel Yfremov, left Paris, probably via Oslo, with an envelope of instructions" said Gretel. " It was decided to release Yfremov so that, from here in Stockholm, he can be followed and discovered the entire network. Possibly Yfremov is about to arrive.

Max Kropelin left the sofa and took a few steps into the small room. His broad forehead had wrinkled, denoting the strain of his brain. Gretel thought that he looked very little like the shoulder she had seen on the night before, a somewhat carefree fellow, very animated by the prospect of a possible conquest, and with the appearance of any Swedish workman.

Max Kropelin now looked like a man, ready to fight.

"What else do you know about this Yfremov?" Max asked suddenly, looking straight at Gretel.

"He is a man over forty years old; dark hair; something thick, looking like a merchant from any country, including Germany.

Max laughed dryly.

"Perfect. The Russians know how to choose, their men "said." Do you think that with this information we have a high probability of success?

Gretel shrugged.

"Horst said you did.

"Horst Anthelme overvalues me," growled Max. Anyway, I suppose there is no alternative but to look for Yfremov. It is too valuable a piece for us to argue. You say you are about to arrive?

"Yes.

"Isn't there a possibility that it has arrived?

"There is a possibility, of course," Gretel said.

Without further ado, turning his back on that woman, Max Kropelin went to the telephone, located on a small table cornered in the room. Quickly, as he sucked in the cigarette smoke, he dialed a number.

He waited impatiently for a few moments. When he noticed that they were picking up on the other side, he inquired:

"Kurbjuhn?

"Middle Kurbjuhn. The other medium stayed in Germany "answered a voice." When do we return, Max?

"Listen," growled Max, ignoring that question "; How about a walk to my house?

"Now?

"Why not?" Growled Max.

"Well ... Anyway, I wanted to talk to you about something. Max. I will take the opportunity. What kind of drink do you have?

"I don't drink," Max grumbled. You know, that is left to the Nazis.

There was a giggle on the other end of the thread.

"Always so bitter, Max," Kurbjuhn said.

"Don't delay," said Max.

"Don't hang up!" Kurbjuhn yelled.

"What happens now?" Asked Max.

"A few hours ago a guy who signed up as Jean Maurvalier arrived at the hotel« Malnihöus », where I work; French name, as you can see, It is, therefore, a potential enemy. I have tried to be the one to carry your luggage, a simple suitcase, to your room. This one was not very good, and, with my ear to the door, I heard something that may be interesting: the guy has mumbled seaweed, in Russian. How about? The bad thing is that my shift was over and I had to go home,

Max licked his lips and glanced at Gretel, who was watching him, very still, silent,

"What was that man Kurbjuhn like?" Asked Max.

"Well ... It's easy to describe: small, stocky, with that confidence of a wealthy merchant, used to traveling. He looks a little over forty years old "Kurbjuhn replied,

Max took a deep breath.

"Perfect" he growled. I'll be waiting for you in fifteen minutes.

He hung up the phone - and took a few steps toward Gretel. He stared at her in silence for a few seconds, without, of course, disregarding his well-curved, very white knees.

"We may have achieved something," he said. A stroke of luck, naturally. Anyway, let's hope Kurbjuhn arrives.

Max sat on the couch next to Gretel and closed his eyes briefly. A hint of a smile curved her lips. He was with a beautiful woman, yes. It is true that women only report complications. There was no love date there. Actually, there was not even a woman as such; Gretel was the ally. Besides, Max had definitely been wrong about her: she was a real iceberg.

It was very difficult to see that white face, thin, but attractive, exotic, with almost half the side of the face hidden by dark hair.

"You can go, Gretel," said, at last, Max. Or has it not fulfilled its mission?

The woman stared at Max.

"It is not true that the first impression is good" he said, puzzling Max a bit,

"What do you mean?" Inquired the German.

"At first, I was afraid Horst was wrong about you. However, now, he is only able to think about his work.

Max shrugged.

"I don't know how ridiculous I would make myself try again to push things to a more ... intimate ground," growled Max.

"Try it.

Max looked into her eyes; Gretel remained motionless, her back erect, giving a new, different air to that room in Max Kropelin's bachelor apartment; giving it an air of enigma, of adventure that was worth savoring.

Max moved closer to her and put his hands on the woman's shoulders. Then, he brought his lips to Gretel's. The woman's reaction, once their lips had met, did not surprise him at all. He felt it vibrate. Then, as Gretel's hands gently rested on the back of Max's neck, his long, muscular arms gently encircled her back.

It was a long, intense kiss.

When he released Gretel, Max said:

"This is better, Gretel. You have mystified me one more time: the last one.

"We'll get to know each other a little better, Max. I thought it was worth it ", smiled Gretel, as she extended her hand, clearing the German's forehead of a blond lock of hair.

"You might be disappointed," Max muttered.

Gretel looked Max in the eye. He saw virility, strength, contained energy. Also a bit of bitterness.

"No," Gretel whispered.

"It is easy to be wrong in our circumstances. "Said Max." Anyway, you didn't answer my question. Did you end up here in Stockholm?

"Yes.

"In that case you must go back to Germany," said Max.

"No, Max.

"Are you afraid to go back?" Asked the German.

"It's not that. Let's say I found something I was looking for "answered, serenely, Gretel". You can't help a certain selfishness in any circumstance, Max. From here I can also be useful to Germany ... with less risk; I don't have to deny that. And Horst will be fine without me.

Max felt a slight emptiness in his stomach. He was about to respond when Gretel's lips pressed against his. Certainly women have very compelling means of achieving anything.

In those moments, a weak knock sounded on the door of the apartment.

Max broke away from Gretel and walked over to his jacket, wielding a pistol that he pulled from an inside pocket. He went to the door.

He remained a little undecided, since he perceived, quite clearly, the heavy breathing of the man who insisted on calling.

He made up his mind to open it at last, stepping aside as he pulled on the wooden blade. She jumped sharply when the man leaning on it flung open as the door slid open, filling it, almost immediately, with blood.

Max reacted quickly, closing the door. Then, eagerly, he leaned next to the man, turning his face. He saw a livid face that seemed scarred by death.

"Kurbjuhn," Max muttered.

The man opened his mouth, but only managed to let out a mouthful of blood, which soaked the front of his shirt, and his dark tie. Kurbjuhn's eyes twisted wildly in their sockets, and the veins in his neck bulged, perhaps making an effort to say something. He did it in an almost unintelligible way.

"They... followed me, Max...

"The Gestapo?" Asked Max, quickly, noticing that tiny drops of cold sweat were born on his forehead,

"Nerd...

"Jean Maurvalier?

"You ... I suspect ... yes ...

"Up to here?" Max asked.

Kurbjuhn shook his head, gasping for air. He was drenched in sweat, and strands of gray hair were stuck to his forehead, very cold, marbled. It seemed that, suddenly, his eyes had sunk into the sockets.

"I don't think ... I could ... I could throw them off, Max ..." he stammered.

"More than one?" Asked Max.

Kurbjuhn nodded.

Then, abruptly, his neck seemed to snap, and the man's head hung to the right, limp, without strength, without any nerve to support it. Slowly Max lowered the body to the ground, biting his lower lip furiously.

Who was to blame for that death? Hadn't Kurbjuhn always been an honest, peaceful man, brimming with humanity?

When Gretel reached Max, she saw that Max's fists were clenched; face twitching; the broad forehead glistening with sweat. When Max looked at Gretel she was about to back away, startled by the expression in Max's blue-gray pupils.

"Go back to your hotel, Gretel" he said dryly.

"As you wish, Max ...

"Wait!" Growled Max. You can do better. I cannot leave Kurbjuhn's corpse here indefinitely. I need you to rent a car and park it right in front of the entrance of this building. You have understood?

"Of course.

***

Bearing the weight of the corpse, Max waited for Gretel's signal that he could see perfectly inside the car, parked according to Max's instructions. When Gretel made the sign, it meant that no one was on the street right now.

Max, gathering strength, almost ran in the direction of the car, while the woman opened the door corresponding to the rear seats. There, anyway, and muttering a "I'm sorry, Kurbjuhn," Max deposited the body of his companion. Then, quickly, when the engine of the German export car was snoring, Max got into the car, next to Gretel, slamming the door.

Gretel, behind the wheel, inquired:

"And now, Max?

"Look for any lonely place by the sea," Max replied.

The car started at good speed, heading east of the city, where any place would be good to make a corpse disappear.

"We can't risk the Swedish police finding him and making inquiries," Max explained. We also run the risk of the news reaching the ears, which would be very easy, even from the newspapers, of the Gestapo agents in Stockholm. That would be as much as putting them on the trail of our anti-Nazi group.

"It's easy to understand," said Gretel.

A few minutes later, the girl stopped the car next to a lonely cliff. Max got out and took Kurbjuhn's body. He carried it all the way to the sea. It would be difficult to recover, since the easiest thing was for it to remain between the rocks. In any case, it would take them a long time to find out, since this was not a place suitable for swimming; as for the fishing barges, they never went near the rocks.

Max returned to the car.

He leaned back in the seat next to Gretel, without saying a word. The woman took the address of Stockholm without prior consultation, and determined to respect Max's silence.

The German lit a cigarette and smoked, staring blankly.

"Kurbjuhn was the one who extended his hand to me when, after my desertion, I managed to reach Switzerland," Max whispered at last. He was there then and together we moved north to do our work. Kurbjuhn always said that he had left Germany and would one day return. One more that won't make it.

Gretel, without looking at the man, inquired:

"Why the Wehrmacht desertion, Max?

"Why?" Repeated, with a strange smile, Max. It can be explained in a few words: He could not bear the murders of the SS and the "Einsatzgruppen"; they razed what the army left standing. That is to say: women and children. Any peasant was, for them, the most dangerous of the guerrillas. I have seen thousands of people die, en masse, in a few minutes. Jews ... So what? I don't know how human Dr. Becker is either. I am referring to an SS commander, a scientist, who made the great discovery of the "S" trucks ...

Gretel shivered at the dry, obviously false laugh of Max Kropelin.

"The 'S' trucks ..." Max repeated. I can never forget it! Never! It's been more than ten months since I saw the last one and I still haven't managed to close my eyes without seeing the show ... The "S" trucks ...

The "S" trucks were closed vehicles and built in such a way that when the engine was started the gases penetrated inside the box, causing the death, in a time of ten or fifteen minutes, to the prisoners. Women and children traveled in this class of trucks, and this kind of death was devised to make mass executions more bearable for the SS, since many of them were married, with children, and protests were raised for the death. The fact of being forced to the "moral torture" of shooting women and children, who were deceived, assuring them that they were going to a concentration camp. As can be seen, the idea only tended to favor the executioners, since in this way they were relieved from confronting defenseless groups with their weapons. Subsequently, some drivers of the "S" trucks complained,

"I'm sorry I told you about this, Max," Gretel murmured.

"Don't worry," the German said dryly. Besides that I can't forget it, I also don't want that to happen. At least as long as the Nazi party owns Germany. Did you know that I was in Rovno, in the hospital, with a minor injury, when the raid on a block of empty men's houses? At the most, there were fifty or sixty elders. I saw them dragging the corpses of their grandchildren ... The concrete answer to the reason for my-desertion is: I don't want to be a monster, Gretel.

"I understand, Max" the girl whispered, directing a fleeting glance at the man, whose face was still drawn and sweaty.

Max tried to compose himself and said:

"To Hotagen Street, Gretel. There is the hotel where Kurbjuhn worked.

Gretel asked no questions. Actually, that reaction from Max had suspected her.

"Are you planning to get something? -" is the only thing he asked.

"Jean Maurvalier is staying there; I suspect it is Yfremov himself, and he is no stranger to Kurbjuhn's murder.

They did not speak anymore; the car slid down the avenues and bridges that connect the small islands, towards Hotagen Street, located near the nightstand where Max and the girl had met, and where Max had met Kurbjuhn on a few occasions.

Max had lit another cigarette and was feeling calmer as he approached the hotel. The German knew very well that a failure of his nerves could cost him his life, and perhaps something else since he always had one thing in mind: he was also fighting against the Gestapo. More than once Max wondered what his worst enemy was.

"We're coming, Gretel, slow down now," Max ordered, two blocks from the hotel.

Gretel obeyed, pulling the car to the sidewalk, lonely at this time of night. There were a few lights that were flickering, giving the dark road a glow.

The girl looked at Max and asked:

"Do you think I could help you, Max?

"You must disappear" growled the German. What if they eliminated me too?

"Well ... the Soviet network would still be intact ...

"As long as something happens to you, Gretel" cut off Max. " If I fall there are others in Stockholm, Remember this name: Oto Giessemann; and her address: Lüdvika, 33. And remember also that you must take care of yourself.

"Yes, Max.

Max was about to leave the car, but he stopped for a moment, looking at Gretel's lips, who had moved her face forward and was looking for Max's gaze.

The German leaned down and placed his lips on Gretel's. Shortly after, without saying a word, he would walk away in the direction of the hotel, leaving the woman with a serious, serene expression, but with a slight stirring in her chest.

3

Max Kropelin entered the hotel. The "Malnihöus" was second-rate, low-key, but clean and with acceptable service. The building was three stories high, massive, ornate, old.

There were very few people in the lobby at the moment and they paid no attention to anyone. Max ye headed, towards the reception desk, behind which stood a young man with bleached blond hair,

"Room for tonight," Max said.

The blond slid a discreet glance towards Max's place, no doubt looking for the luggage.

Max smiling, clarified:

"I have no luggage. I will pay for my accommodation in advance, naturally.

The young man nodded and opened the record book, which was a way like any other to ask for identification documents, Max rubbed a card, provided by Horst Anthelme himself, on which it read: Rhudy Carlsen, from thirty-two years old, from Malmö.

The only certainty of those data was the age.

As the receptionist wrote down the details in the ledger, Max slid his penetrating gaze over the other names recorded in the volume, not taking long to find Jean Maurvalier's. Second floor, room 27.

Soon after, Max was alone in room 38, on the top floor.

He lit a cigarette and walked to the wide window, peering outside. He sighed, disappointed. From there it would be impossible to reach the flat of Maurvalier or Yfremov. Therefore, you should use a much more direct method: introduce yourself through the door of the room.

It took him a few minutes to decide, thinking that Maurvalier was probably not in his room. Maybe they were still looking for Kurbjuhn. This, of course, could make his job easier, since he could make a thorough search of the Russian's luggage.

He left his room and descended the stairs without the slightest stumble. The number 27, stuck to the door of that room, stood out before his eyes.

Max felt the pistol and waited a few seconds, listening for footsteps.

Soon after, he was quickly manipulating the lock. As his forehead began to be dripping with sweat, there came a muffled metallic sound. Max pushed the blade and quickly entered the room. He closed the door and took a flashlight from his pocket.

A quick walk in the beam of light convinced him that the room was empty.

He walked over to a cupboard taped to the right wall and slid the door open. A hanging suit and a suitcase appeared before his eyes. He fingered the suit without hearing the rustle of paper he expected. He remembered very well that Gretel had told him that Yfremov carried an envelope with instructions.

He opened the suitcase, which appeared completely empty.

Max gritted his teeth, grunting a curse. He began feeling the suitcase, to no avail. It was very simple and it was not possible to think of a double bottom. Of course, that had to be checked ...

In those moments, Max was paralyzed, almost blinded by the light, much more intense than that of the flashlight, that had suddenly been made in the room. Then he heard the door to the room quietly close and a voice:

"Do not move. I'm targeting you.

Max stood still, tense, attentive to that click approaching him. A woman. A woman with a strange foreign accent and a somewhat hoarse, thick, suggestive voice, but also harsh.

What were you looking for here? Who are you? "Asked the woman.

Max turned with a smile. A look of astonishment leapt into his eyes when he saw the woman.

She was tall, with a swaying body, tight by a dark dress, although it was not as dark as her hair, very black, shiny, very long. The woman's eyes, also black, were slanted and pointed slightly upward, which gave the impression that some of the woman's ancestry was Asian; Mongolian, perhaps.

His mouth was red, a little big; the lips were tight now.

"Well ..." Max started. My name is Rhudy Carlsen, and I was briefed on Mr. Maurvalier's portfolio. I thought it was worth trying pocket change for some bills. We have bad times, you know.

The woman was unmoved; no gesture; he was still holding a pistol steadily.

"You don't look like a hotel pickpocket, Carlsen," he said, in that deep, thick voice.

"Thank you, Madame," he said. The truth is that I have not always been. But in the face of hunger ...

"Shut up!

Max shrugged.

"Okay," he grunted. Call the police.

The woman blinked, which brought a mocking laugh from Max.

"Or are you not interested in the intervention of the police? "Inquired the German-". You are Russian, right?

The woman seemed uneasy; He showed it by the slight twitching of his pistol hand. He did not answer Max's question. Just said:

"I'm going to do better than call the police. Turn your back.

Max turned, slowly; but with all his senses tense, waiting for his chance. This came when the woman took two steps forward and raised her armed arm.

Max turned fiercely, no longer a trace of a smile, and managed to half-dodge the blow; She wedged it into her shoulder, but the pain, very bearable, did not prevent the woman from suddenly opening her mouth wide and making an effort not to let out a howl of pain, when Max's fingers gripped her arm. .

The German let go of her abruptly and snatched the pistol from her. Max's second action was to slap the woman violently, and she took several steps back, until she stumbled on the bed.

She stood there, panting, furious, before Max, who had drawn his own pistol and was advancing on the woman.

"Where is Yfremov?" He inquired dryly.

The woman, who was calming down, only said:

"Yfremov?

Max smiled coldly. He came closer to the Russian, grabbing her by the hair; He pulled back forcing the woman to raise her face high.

"Do you think I would mind killing her?" Max whispered. You are not unaware that in the kind of struggle we have chosen there are no concessions.

"Shoot," said the woman laconically.

Max laughed.

"No. Not here, at least "he said. Were you the link that should receive Yfremov? Was it you who discovered Kurbjuhn?

"Yes.

Max nodded.

"Kurbjuhn is dead," he said. I knew it?

"I imagined it. I see you had time to communicate with someone.

"Maybe a little late ... for him, of course" growled Max. Anyway, we know that a man's life is of very little importance today. Nor does a woman more or less matter.

"I do care about mine" said the woman.

"I understand. Does that mean she's willing to talk? - "Max asked.

"Yes.

The German sighed.

"Perfect. Make yourself comfortable, "she said, letting go of her hair.

The Russian, very serene, understood by making herself comfortable the fact of positioning herself so that Max could contemplate the shape of her knees, which, briefly, made the German remember Gretel. The Russian, of course, had nothing to envy Gretel. She had sat on the bed, crossing her legs, so that Max, to face her, turned his back to the bedroom door, "I don't do this for money," the woman began. " I managed to escape from a concentration camp. I could not return to Russia nor did I dare to stay in Eastern Europe. My solution was in a neutral country: Sweden. It took me a long time to get to Stockholm, "she said, bowing her head, as if embarrassed by something she had been forced to do.

Max didn't flinch. The Russian was blatantly lying; of that he was totally convinced. That woman was a professional spy,

"Go ahead," said Max.

"-Once in Stockholm, I received a visit from a man who proposed to me to act in small liaison missions of no importance, but which would allow me to live with some ease and, furthermore, with the satisfaction of those who know that it is useful,

"Who is that man?" Asked Max.

"I do not know. They haven't trusted me much. I receive orders in the most unexpected places and when I begin to believe that they have forgotten me. This time I received the order to wait for Yfremov at this hotel and serve as a link to reach them. I just did it. The rest of my mission is to wait to be ordered to change residence, as on any other occasion. I heard you picking the lock and stupidly intervened. That's it, roughly speaking.

"What's your name?" Asked Max.

"Sonia Yourskof.

"Didn't you know about Yfremov's mission either?

"No.

Max laughed.

"Finally; Do you think I have swallowed a single one of your words? "He asked, stopping laughing and approaching Sonia furiously". For example: To put Yfremov in contact with others, what did he do?

The Russian lightly pursed her lips.

"Okay," said Max. Let's go.

"Where to?

"With me. To my house. It is much more discreet than a hotel. Come on, "growled Max.

Sonia abandoned her useless posture and stood up. Without saying a word she started toward the bedroom door, followed by the furious German.

The woman opened the door and went out into the hall. When Max was about to do the same, he was painfully surprised by a blow from the barrel of a pistol to the fingers of his right hand. Her gun bounced off the floor and a foot hit her, sending her toward the back of the room.

Then, when Max still had not managed to react, a fist slammed into his stomach forcing him to bend over, aching, dazed. A blow to the forehead threw him back.

In a thick mist, he saw the man who, after entering the room, was closing the door.

Both were left there alone, while Sonia had disappeared.

"Gestapo? "The guy muttered,

"No.

"Oh ... one of those unhappy anti-Nazis" smiled that man, plump, a little bald and almost good-natured face. " You lack organization or, what amounts to the same thing, strength. How did you manage to discover me in Paris?

"We may not be as weak as you suppose, Yfremov," said Max, who was recovering from the blows.

"Anyway, you guys are fighting for something I hate, you understand?" Muttered the Russian, his face tightening, which took on an unsuspected hardness.

"That's not true," growled Max. Communism thrives on guys like you. It is not about hatred, but about system.

Yfremov laughed again.

"We will not discuss that now," he said. Open the window.

Max frowned. He stared at the pistol the Soviet agent was holding. Very well. Open the window.

As the rush of cool, damp air entered the room, Max took a deep breath. Suddenly, he froze, realizing what Yfremov was up to. His pores opened, letting thick beads of sweat trickle down that seemed to freeze on the German's body.

"Jump," ordered the Russian dryly. With a bit of luck he can be saved.

That was a one in a thousand chance, and Yfremov knew it perfectly well. Hence its slightly ironic tone.

"Is there someone else downstairs?" Asked Max, desperately stalling for time.

"Of course.

"Understand. They will finish me off with two shots to the back of my neck and they will quickly make my body disappear "said Max.

"You are smart," Yfremov smiled. Jump?

Max took a deep breath. He quickly calculated his chances of getting out of this situation. He immediately ruled out the somersault to the street. However, a bullet, if it succeeded in disconcerting Yfremov, could be only mild. In any case, he would fight.

The German tensed his muscles and flexed his legs slightly. I would jump, yes, but ...

Against what he expected, Yfremov did not fire. It seemed that the Russian was expecting that reaction, since he quickly stepped aside, while shooting his right foot against Max's chin. However, Yfremov was surprised by the violence displayed by Max, who even managed to deflect the blow, grabbing the Russian's foot with both hands.

Max gave a silent laugh that raised the hair of his enemy, who could not help but lose his balance and fall backwards. After the body hit the ground, another one resounded, slightly sharp, and it was Yfremov's crown on the ground as a result of a savage punch delivered by Max to the full nose.

The German sat up, looking for the pistol on the ground. However, when he reached out his hand, his fingers were pinned to the ground, crushed by the foot of the Russian, who was beginning to rise.

Max, through clenched teeth, elbowed furiously into the Russian's stomach, who let out a hoarse groan and fell onto his side.

However, it seemed to bounce surprising Max, who could not believe that this little man could display such energy.

When he remembered that it was a Soviet agent, he had already received a punch in the chest and another in the chin, which forced him to go back to the window, being framed in it.

Yfremov jumped towards him, reaching out with both hands and grabbing onto the German's neck.

Gasps began to flow. Sweat trickled down the faces of both men in bright streaks. Max's was beginning to show a purple color that was increasing in tone.

Finally, Max managed to raise his right knee, driving it into Yfremov's lower abdomen. His hands seemed to gain more strength, as if he were trying to mitigate the pain by grasping something, Of course that something was Max's neck, who savagely repeated the blow,

And he noticed, immediately, that he could breathe almost normally, as Yfremov released the pressure on his throat.

Anxiously, Max gulped in air and leaned over, almost squatting, so that his head was pressed against the Russian's stomach. Abruptly he stood up, lifting Yfremov, who, in a second, and at Max's movement with his arms, pushing him backwards, went through the window frame, plunging into the void.

There was a bloodcurdling scream and, seconds later, a dull shock, forcing Max to close his eyes briefly. He had fleetingly imagined that he might have been the one to hit the road.

Without looking at the street, he ran to the door of the room when rumors began to sound outside.

With the pistol in his hand, he looked for a moment for Sonia with his eyes. Useless. Sonia had disappeared and he didn't have much time to waste there.

Quickly, he gained the third floor and snuck into his room. Without turning on the light, he looked down through the window and saw a strange sight.

Two armed men had rushed towards Yfremov. After a short hesitation, one of them charged the body, running towards a car parked a short distance from the hotel door, while the other, also backing away, kept the people who were beginning to arrive and an employee at bay with his pistol. of the hotel that had appeared at the door.

Only seconds later an engine was snoring and the car sped away at impressive speed.

Max, furious, clenched his fists.

And the damn Sonia?

Well ... It would appear. The important thing in those moments was to leave the hotel undisturbed. The Swedish police would arrive and want to know a lot about the guests.

4

The easiest thing was to go from the roof of the hotel to the one of the adjoining building. Max descended the stairs and reached the street, disappearing from those contours.

He walked quickly, though not enough to attract attention, until he found a bar. A minute later he was inside the phone booth waiting for an answer to his call.

"Say," a voice sounded.

"I'll wait for you at my house, Otto" growled Max. " Get out right now.

"What's wrong, Max?" Asked the other.

"It is a bit long to explain. This is something important; something that is really worth it.

"Good, I'm glad. It was about time we were good for more than just poking around stupidly or continually sneaking out of the Gestapo. I'm going there, Max.

They hung up, Max went out into the street and I started walking, thinking furiously of his bad luck. Yfremov had disappeared, just like Sonia, which made things difficult or, at least, delayed the moment of working seriously against the Soviet sabotage network.

As for the instruction envelope, it was already stupid to think about it, since Yfremov had managed to deliver it to his companions.

Max crossed almost deserted streets until he reached the shipyards, from where you could see the windows of his house. He was in a hurry to find out if the men who chased Kurbjuhn had made it there or lost track of him altogether, as it seemed at first glance.

Then he smiled slightly, remembering the rush the Russians had taken to rescue Yfremov's body. Actually, that kind of struggle, deaf, dark, contained all kinds of dangers, beginning with going mad with fear.

Three minutes later, Max was in front of his door. He opened and turned on the light.

He immediately heard a sigh of relief and saw the man with the gun.

"I was beginning to worry, Max," Otto Giessemann growled. I thought you called me from here.

Without responding, Max glanced down the hall and then walked into the inner rooms, checking that nothing had been touched. This meant that the Russians had not been able to follow Kurbjuhn there, which was a relief.

When he got to the living room, Max lit a cigarette, and Otto exploded:

"But what the hell is going on?" He inquired.

Max stared at him and growled:

Sit down, Otto.

Giessemann obeyed. This was a tall, massive man with imposing muscles and a shrewd brain. His head was almost square, blond; short hair, with some premature graying, since Otto was about Max's age.

Max, taking short walks around the room, explained what had happened since they had arrived at his house that night accompanied by Gretel, ending when he saw the car that was transporting the busted Yfremov flee.

"Kurbjuhn ...-" Otto whispered. I can't believe it, Max.

"Stop fooling around," growled Max. As you can see, we have lost the possibility of finishing earlier, since Yfremov died without me being able to make him loosen his tongue. Therefore, we only have one clue to follow and it will not be easy: Sonia.

"We will waste a lot of time," Otto grumbled. Instead of these people, I would keep Sonia in a display case until the sabotage they are preparing had been carried out.

"You can do more," said Max. For example: find out what ships are going to Germany with a cargo of steel, do you understand? If we own the list of those ships, we are likely to be able to prevent them from being sabotaged. Of course we will have to mobilize several of our men.

Otto nodded.

"What system do they use to fly the ships? He inquired.

"I don't know!" Growled Max.

Otto sighed slightly and stood up.

"Okay, Max. Tonight we will get moving. I wonder if this will do any good in relation to the war, I mean if it will help it to end sooner, "he said.

"Who knows?

"That's the worst: the uncertainty," muttered Otto. " I'd give anything to be able to return tomorrow. I lived very well on my farm, really. Did you know that before I moved to the Russian front, we received as a maid a beautiful Polish girl, Max?

Max smiled slightly.

"You have explained it many times, Otto" he said "; She has the biggest eyes you've ever seen and she's strong, sweet, and submissive. You would marry her with your eyes closed and you swore to your brother that you would kill him if something happened to her.

Otto's eyes, very clear, flashed.

"That's right," he growled. I will give back to the girl what she has lost. I don't like slavery, Max.

Max set his jaws.

"Okay," he said. We'll come back one day, Otto. Meanwhile, we must continue fighting. This is a good opportunity to convince the anti-Nazis in hiding that we can do something, as long as we unite.

"By that you mean to get out of here and get to work, right?" Otto growled.

"Exactly.

The two men started walking in the direction of the apartment door. They stopped suddenly, hearing a sound of footsteps approaching the door,

Max's reaction was immediate. He beckoned Otto to hide and turned off the light, just as a timid knock sounded on the door.

Max smiled strangely and, pistol in his right hand, opened the door, stepping aside.

"Gretel ..." he muttered in amazement.

The woman seemed relieved to see Max.

"I thought something had happened to you, Max," he said, penetrating the floor. " I have been to the "Malnihöus" before deciding to come here.

Max frowned,

"Well?" He inquired.

"I have discovered something important.

"Agree. We will talk.

Otto had reappeared and Max made the introductions briefly. The three returned to the living room.

Gretel took the sofa and Otto sat down in a chair. Max took his preferred position, facing. window.

"I didn't leave you alone, Max," began Gretel. " I advanced the car a little more, approaching the hotel. I thought it might be a useless waste of time waiting for you there, when a car arrived and a woman got out on her way to the hotel. Maybe it was a hunch, but I decided to keep waiting, watching the other three occupants of the vehicle, who after ten minutes began to show impatience. A man descended... Was it Yfremov? "Inquired Gretel.

Max took a deep breath.

"It was Yfremov," he said.

"Yeah" grinned Gretel. Shortly after, that same man was thrown out of a window and I was surprised by the attitude of the others, who rushed to retrieve the body, disappearing from there. A few minutes before that woman had reappeared and got into the car. When it started, I started mine.

"Perfect," Max muttered. " Did you follow them?

"Yes. Even a house located on the outskirts, very close to the sea "said Gretel" I told myself that the best thing would be to let you know. When I couldn't find you at the hotel, after some very discreet questions, I began to think about the possibility that something had happened to you.

Max smiled and looked at Otto,

"We have been lucky," he said. Let's see, Gretel- Was there someone in that house?

"I do not know. I didn't think it was wise to get too close. Anyway, there was no light.

"That doesn't mean anything," growled Max. The really important thing, therefore, is not to miss this opportunity to eliminate this Soviet group. In these moments we could be successful, They do not suspect that they have been followed.

"Are you thinking of going there?" Otto inquired.

"As simple as that,

"We alone?" Otto inquired.

"I don't think there are more than three of them," answered Max. "On the other hand, we have the surprise in our favor. Walking.

A few minutes later they were settled in the car Gretel had rented. She got behind the wheel and Max next to her. Otto settled into the back seats.

The car started and they drove through the first few minutes in silence. Gretel cut it off.

"It's strange, Max" he murmured "When I lost sight of you in the hotel I started to feel that something was missing and I was afraid, do you believe me?

Max looked at her; He could only see the outline of the exotic face of the woman, who had spoken without looking at Max, staring at the asphalt. He noticed Gretel's thin lips, her long lashes.

"Why not?" Max mused. You always expect something like this to happen. When he arrives, he is surprised. We are somewhat demoralized, Gretel, and we cling to anything that can bring us back to the reality that life goes on. One of those things is love.

"Love ..." Gretel whispered.

Otto, from behind, caught that whisper and shuddered. He remembered the Polish girl with the big eyes and the sweet look. Damn war! He loved her and had to be away from her. At the very least, Max was luckier, since Gretel was there. Many things lose importance when something as intense as a newborn love is involved.

Otto's love for the Polish slave was also newborn, tormenting.

He remembered very well the day the SS awarded it to his farm, to the Giessemann farm, all belonging to the Nazi party, including Otto, until he made his first weapons on the Russian border. There he began to feel horror of the war, the SS and even himself. He managed to flee from there. Someday, if that exile took too long, he would go to Germany to find the Pole.

"There is light in the house" said the girl. It is the second on the left of the road.

Max quickly calculated the distance and ordered:

Slow down, Gretel. The rest we can cover very well on foot.

The car left the road, into the open field, behind a group of trees.

* * *

A powerful flashlight illuminated that strange cave. Two men, in silence, tense, without their faces expressing anything at all, changed their clothes, not caring at all about the presence of a woman, a beautiful Russian who held the lantern.

Within minutes, these men were crammed into their dark rubber suits, their hands bare and their faces smeared.

In the cave, cornered, there was an inflatable boat, with just enough capacity for two people. In another corner was a wooden box full of strange artifacts. There was also a small arsenal, consisting of submachine guns and hand grenades.

"Ready, Sonia" sounded a voice.

The woman walked a few steps into the tunnel, while one of those men took the boat, and the other, some of the artifacts that were in the wooden box.

They followed Sonia, who projected the ray of light on the humid earth of the tunnel.

Shortly after they reached the bottom of the tunnel, and between the two men, after momentarily putting their artifacts on the ground, they spun a rock, just enough so that their bodies could slide through the opening.

After a considerable effort from both of them, the rock moved and the cave came, immediately, the cool and humid breeze from the sea and the unmistakable smell of saltpeter.

You could hear the sound of the waves crashing against the cliff and some particles of sprayed water penetrated through that hole.

One of those men released the boat, which immediately swelled, coming to rest between some rocks. Then one of the fellows descended, retrieving it, and reaching out to conveniently position the artifacts that extended from the opening.

Shortly after, the boat, with the two men and their explosive charge, was moving silently into the waters of the Baltic.

They had previously plugged the hole from the outside with a heavy rock prepared for the purpose.

Sonia, calm, lit up for the return, moving away from there.

He came to some rough dirt stairs and ascended. Pushing with both arms he raised a trap with a carpet and turned on the light in that room.

He went to the phone, hanging on the wall, a few steps from the window of that room, which overlooked the sea, dark, disturbing.

He took the device and dialed a number. When they answered the call, Sonia said:

"Ready.

"By when?" Inquired a voice.

"Thing of half an hour; maybe less "said Sonia.". You can?

There was a hoarse laugh, somewhat sarcastic,

"Whatever," said that voice then. " What happened to this Yfremov?

"Dead" replied Sonia.

"Will that affect anything?

"I do not think so. At the moment, only I am known by an anti-Nazi agent "Sonia replied". Anyway, we will have work after this, you understand? It could be dangerous to let that agent search.

"Already. We will anticipate him, right?

"If possible.

"It has to be. It has to be done. You already know, Sonia. We are doing a great job and we don't have to give it up without a fight.

Sonia pursed her lips.

"I don't like your sarcasm," he said through his teeth. It's true: it has to be done. You said it before: whatever. Understood? And naturally, this position we will not abandon without a fight. It took too long to get here.

"I know, I know...

"I don't like your indifference" Sonia said.

A mocking laugh rang out.

"Are you afraid that I will betray the group?" Asked the man, on the other side of the thread.

"Well ... I just want to remind you of something: The Nazis are pushing us into Russia at a rate that I would not be surprised by anything that would place them at the gates of Moscow. Do you know what that would represent? And do you know what their advancement represents? Hundreds of thousands of our people are dying and their death camps are filling with bodies of Russians. What do you say to that?

"Any. Already knew. We cannot stop that advance, but perhaps the American material will. It is reaching thousands of tons.

"I prefer to trust ourselves," Sonia grumbled. " Don't linger anymore.

"It's okay. What are you going to do?

"Rest," Sonia murmured, a grimace of exhaustion appearing on her face. " At least, until they return; it will take a long time.

"Already. Bye.

They hung up the phone and Sonia went to a box on a table, from which she extracted a cigarette. She lit it and smoked for a moment, thoughtful, her clear white forehead crossed by a vertical crease.

At last, he slowly made his way to his room. She lay clothed on the bed, her eyes wide and dark. Only the ember of the cigarette glowed from time to time.

In his mind, he mapped out the route of the inflatable boat in the direction of the city harbor. It was an obvious advantage to work at a neutral point.

Shortly after, he was looking for the ashtray and stubbed out the cigarette butt. He closed his eyes thinking that maybe he could sleep.

<h1 style="text-align:center">5</h1>

Sonia opened her eyes suddenly startled. He pricked up his ears and noticed quite clearly the noise someone makes when picking at a lock with a fake key.

He jumped out of bed and stood motionless for a moment, biting his lip.

There was only one solution that could be reached: the fact that there, outside, someone was trying to enter the house did not mean anything good.

Sonia left her room and slipped silently, in the dark, in the direction of the one in which the trap that led to the tunnel was located. Confused ideas crowded into his brain. How had that happened? Who would have discovered them?

Furious, she opened the trap and placed the carpet so that when the wood was lowered it was completely flat on the floor, hiding the trap. It did so at the moment when there was a metallic click, indicating that the lock had given.

Flashlight in hand, he ran to the bottom of the tunnel. There were automatic weapons there, or at any rate he could try to flee through the hole.

The woman, her forehead beaded with sweat, took a submachine gun and stood with her back to the opening, pressing to see if at any given moment this could be her escape point.

The sweat rose when he realized that this effort was totally useless. The rock placed outside, plugging the hole, had not moved at all.

He remembered very well that the two men who had left shortly before resorted to a hard joint effort to move.

He closed his eyes for a moment and told himself to calm down. After all, they hadn't discovered her yet, and she had a submachine gun in her hands.

He turned off the flashlight and stood in a corner, motionless, his eyes wide in the dark.

A strange smile folded his lips, thinking that a burst in time, by surprise, could save him much trouble.

* * *

The door gave way and Max Kropelin stepped inside. Otto and Gretel followed, each holding pistols and all senses tense.

"Maybe there will be a surprise," Max whispered. "There must be someone, since the light has not turned off by itself. And no one has left the house after.

They waited a few moments to get used to the darkness and to get an idea of the layout of the house.

A faint feminine scent reached Max's nostrils. He glanced toward a half-open door at the back of the house. He smiled slightly, remembering very well what Sonia smelled like when they stumbled into the "Malnihöus."

"Cover the other doors, Otto," Max muttered. You don't move from here, Gretel.

Without waiting for an answer, Max began to advance towards Sonia's room, without using his flashlight. Actually, that began to seem strange, since, according to Gretel's statement, there were at least two men in that house, and Sonia slept with the door open. This was a bit difficult for Max to assimilate, so he was extremely cautious and mentally asked Otto to do the same.

When they reached the door of the room, the perfume of the Russian intensified.

Max took a deep breath and silently jumped into the room.

There was no movement in the room and Max, disappointed, seeing the empty bed clearly enough now, grunted in anger.

How was that possible?

He quickly retraced his steps, addressing Otto.

"We are going to examine the other rooms," he said. I wouldn't be surprised if the house had another way out and we were somehow discovered.

In two minutes they examined the three rooms that consisted of this modern building, probably built by a madman or a capricious, almost right on the edge of a dangerous cliff and of little panoramic beauty. It even seemed that the house was not completely finished or there were many construction defects.

"Otto.

"That?

"Something smells strong to me," growled Max.

"What thing?

"This house has been hastily built by the Russians, with permission, of course, to be used as a headquarters for their sabotage operations.

"You may be right," Otto grumbled. That means that there must be something more than what we are seeing, right?

"The safest.

"Agree. We will search "said Otto.

Max was thoughtful for a moment; then he said:

"While you are looking for the exit, which must exist, I will search Sonia's room. Perhaps we will find something interesting; The fact that they have disappeared from here does not necessarily mean that they have discovered us. They may be doing something.

"Good, Max.

While Otto began to search and carefully examine the rooms, Max and Gretel headed towards Sonia's room,

Max took the flashlight from a pocket of his jacket and directed the beam of light in a circular motion around the room, discovering, from the sparse furniture, consisting of the bed, a chair, a nightstand and a tiny dresser, that he had not been mistaken. thinking that this house was an emergency shelter.

"Look in the dresser, Gretel," Max said as he made his way to the nightstand.

Gretel didn't really even need to open a single cabinet drawer. Exclaimed:

"Max!

The German turned quickly and walked over to Gretel, who was holding an envelope in her right hand. Max took it and sighed when he saw the inscription on the envelope; in Russian: «Shoversenno sekretno»

"Good ..." he murmured. I suppose that I am not mistaken: this is the envelope of instructions, which Yfremov carried.

Gretel bit her lower lip thoughtfully as Max set the flashlight on the dresser to open the envelope.

He tore one end and pulled out the contents,

"Damn it!" He muttered, disappointed. What the hell does this mean?

The envelope contained a series of papers... blank. Mere white sheets, without a single line written, Gretel said:

"Maybe it's written in nice ink, Max, 'I hadn't thought of it,' growled the German." Anyway, I begin to distrust that it is so. I can't imagine Sonia forgetting this envelope on the dresser, do you understand? In addition, this makes me suspect many other things. For example: Yfremov knew the instructions by heart and traveled with this envelope, which could save his life, if some enemy, Gestapo or us, settled for him, do you understand?

"Yes. The envelope was a hook that, if it disappeared, when Yfremov carried it, would have warned him that it had been discovered, thereby taking the precautions destined to disappear.

"I think so" grumbled Max- ". Therefore, we now know positively that Yfremov verbally communicated the instructions for the upcoming sabotage. And the fact that this house is empty means, most likely, that things are underway ...

Max had paled and his forehead began to glow.

"We have to do something," he continued, clenching his fists, crumpling the envelope, which he then threw to the ground, furious.

He was about to leave the room, but Gretel stopped him.

"Max.

The German looked into the woman's eyes. By now, Gretel's pupils had lost that air of cold detachment. In the dim light, his face, shaded under high cheekbones, took on another, more youthful expression.

Max waited for Gretel to speak.

"It is not impossible that they discovered us, Max" said Gretel

"Right, it's not impossible," Max replied. And good?

"In this case, it would not be unreasonable to suppose that we have been set up; who are waiting for us in a trap.

Max thought furiously.

"You have to find out anyway," he growled. For fear of a possible trap we are not going to miss this opportunity.

Gretel's bust, in a silent inspiration, tightened the clothes of the dress.

He did not protest at all. Just said:

"I guess you will anyway.

Max smiled and reached out with his right hand, stroking the woman's left cheek, whose skin vibrated.

"You are smart, Gretel. Horst is obviously a man who knows how to choose his allies. Maybe he's starting to worry about your delay.

Gretel smiled and said:

"You must suspect what is happening to me. He was very insistent that you are an extraordinary man, Max.

A grimace of bitterness twisted the young man's lips. Shook his head,

"Poor Horst ..." he whispered. I'm really just unhappy, Gretel. I do this out of circumstance, not because I have the courage, intelligence, and nerves for this profession. And I confess that when I have been most afraid in my life has been in the fulfillment of some espionage missions near the Gestapo. Even when he was fighting in the Kiev region of Ukraine before the Red Army, he was not so scared. No, Gretel, there is nothing extraordinary about me. I already told you that one day you might be disappointed.

Gretel took a step forward and faced Max. He felt a heat coming from his stomach, gently rising up his chest. When his arms went around Gretel's short waist, all that heat passed to his lips, which settled on the woman's.

It was an intense caress; as if they were both trying to retain something that might flee at any moment.

"I love you, Max -" - whispered Gretel. You're extraordinary. And it is extraordinary that we love each other.

"It is..." Max mused.

The German realized that from the most terrifying loneliness of those last few months he had come to possess something, something that could fill a life.

He squeezed Gretel closer, feeling the firmness, the warmth of that young body. He kissed her again, closing his eyes for a moment. He tried not to remember that Gretel was really a body more sacrificed to a cause that was seemingly lost.

"Come on, Gretel" he murmured then "Otto must be waiting.

"Yeah come on. Thank you ... for not speaking, Max "the young woman whispered, with a somewhat broken voice," I have noticed your tension ...

"Shut up!" Max muttered. Let's go.

Gently, he pushed her toward the exit of that room. They went to where they had left Otto.

Otto was not there. He hadn't expected.

***

Otto, frowning, let his flashlight run across the walls of the room. This big, square-headed, blond, dark-eyed German was not very smart, but he was cunning, and he wasn't going to be fooled by the appearance that there was nothing there to suggest an outside exit.

He had already walked through a room and found himself in the one whose window faced the sea.

I could faintly hear the sound of the waves crashing against the cliff. He didn't like the misty, humid environment; he did not like the sea; He was the man of the land, of the farm.

All that disturbed him, gave him the impression that he was far from his own, from what he loved so much. He was very far from the Polish girl ...

Otto shook his head in reaction.

"You would cry like a child," he told himself.

He thought that if the walls were firm, he should search the floor.

It might be a way of wasting time, but it had to be done. Any effort he made brought him a little closer to everything hers.

The light from the flashlight began to search for a groove in the floor tiles, until it was fixed on that carpet that had a slight crease.

Otto walked over there and kicked the rug away. A strange smile twisted his lips at the discovery of the wooden trap.

Perfect. It was down there. There were two circumstances: that they were waiting for having discovered them or that they were not waiting for them.

Anyway, it was best to bring Max up to speed on what he had discovered.

Without touching the trap, he backed away, heading toward the Russian's room, where Gretel and Max were staying.

Apparently, their silent footsteps were not heard by the couple, who continued to kiss, while Otto, a little surprised, watched them from the doorway.

Otto remained there for several seconds, indecisive, very pale, looking, hypnotized, at those bodies that seemed to be one.

At last, he made a decision: as silently as he had come, he withdrew.

Max was lucky. Max was no longer alone and terribly far from his business.

The big man felt a slight choking and then a suspicious sting in his eyes. He was also there because of the circumstances. He was a peaceful man, a great beer drinker and an eternal admirer of everything beautiful, especially when he was a woman ... like the Polish woman. Sweet, young, wretched ...

He pursed his lips and remembered that each triumph brought him a little closer to everything that was so far away.

Resolute, he headed for the trap without a single doubt that Max would come there at the first sign of danger. Max was a great companion. Max had a great future when Nazism disappeared from Germany and from the layer of the earth. Max was the student who never repeated the course.

Otto took a deep breath and leaned over, searching for the indentation in the wood that served to steady his fingers. He pulled gently and the trap began to lift. He tried not to make the slightest noise and lay on the floor, trying to pick up some noise coming from the dark and damp interior of that open mouth on the floor.

Any.

With sweat damp temples, Otto made up his mind.

6

Sonia was glued to a corner and caught the slight clarity that was made in the tunnel when the hatch was opened. The woman's fingers clenched around the submachine gun she wielded. She held her breath and stared toward the tunnel entrance, alert for the next move of what was undoubtedly an enemy.

He gritted his teeth when he saw a thin cone of light projected onto the ground.

She still waited, since she was not entirely sure that it was a single man who was there.

The woman felt the violent beating of her heart. She believed that it was impossible for the advancing man, assuming he was a man, since he could not make out his silhouette yet, not hear those strong throbbing, which she felt in her throat, in her temples ...

Unexpectedly, the beam of light rose, projecting towards the bottom of the tunnel and reaching almost completely to Sonia, who had glued the butt of the submachine gun to her right hip.

A gasp rang out, finding a strange echo in the tunnel, and Sonia pulled the trigger of the weapon.

Otto Geissmann, surprised by that sudden tongue of fire, only had time to exhale a hoarse groan. He had felt a sharp pain in his chest and was forced to take several steps back, letting go of the flashlight, to find that the strength of his fingers had suddenly disappeared.

With the pistol in his right hand he fired twice, probably by reflex. In any case, the bullets only succeeded in dislodging particles of rock and earth from the ceiling.

He found himself sitting on the ground with his back against the poorly carved wall of the tunnel. His eyes, veiled by anguish, by pain, were fixed on the lantern, which was still emitting a beam of light at ground level.

Then that approaching silhouette ...

It was a woman. Otto was not so bad as not to discover that the figure belonged to a woman.

"The Russian ..." he muttered.

Sonia, tense, with her face contracted, with some hair stuck to her forehead, to her face, due to sweat and humidity, arrived next to the wounded man.

"Who are you? How did you get here? He inquired.

Otto, in those moments, the only thing he knew how to do was let out a muffled laugh. Maybe he was laughing at himself. I thought that no matter how much of a hurry Max was, the bullets were much faster.

Infinitely faster.

"I talked!

Sonia's scream made Otto wince. That woman was nervous. Very nervous. At least he must be as scared as Otto himself.

"Have you come alone?" Sonia continued asking.

"Yes ... That ..., that is: just ..." Otto replied.

What was he looking for?

"An envelope" said Otto. I ... I found it ...

"Really?" Laughed the beautiful Sonia unpleasantly.

"Sure ... Very interesting.

"Lie.

The Russian with Mughal features knew immediately that Otto was lying. He could even lie about being alone in the house. There was a means to make him speak.

Without Otto even suspecting the woman's action, Sonia faced the barrel of the submachine gun at Otto's feet and pulled the trigger.

Again that tongue of fire, brief, but intense. A howl of pain was strangled by the sharp clatter of the weapon, which rumbled deafeningly down the tunnel.

Otto looked down at his bloody feet. He felt the pain rise until it produced excruciating pinpricks in his brain.

In those moments there was a muffled sound on the dirt stairs, and Sonia, losing her composure for a few seconds, fired again, while she retreated towards the bottom of the tunnel, until her back was glued to that damn rock that did not give way. I couldn't get out of there ...

* * *

"Max ...

Max was livid, staring at that open trap, like a monstrous mouth.

Hearing Gretel's whisper, he looked at her and said:

"I heard, Gretel. Stay here. I beg you to flee if I am slow to return or do not show signs of life.

Gretel bit her lip, but couldn't stop two tears from coming into her eyes.

"It can't be that long ..." she whispered, addressing herself more than Max himself.

The German stroked the woman's hair, silently. It was enough to look into her eyes.

He started when he heard again that loud sound of the detonations, which seemed to want to escape through the open trap, Max, without waiting any longer, trying with all his might to forget Gretel, who was still looking at him with wide eyes, as if he did not believe that that could happen, he tossed a box of matches down the stairs.

Immediately, a new chain of dry booms followed, which made the German smile harshly.

As soon as the echo of the shots stopped, he descended those stairs, immediately sticking to the earthy wall, directing the barrel of his pistol toward the bottom of the tunnel.

He saw the light shining that illuminated only one wall of the tunnel although it reverberated enough so that that area was illuminated,

Max saw Sonia.

He saw her pressed against the wall, motionless, looking busily for the silhouette of the man who must have been advancing toward the light.

But Max did not advance. He just aimed calmly and pulled the trigger. For two times. The double boom sounded almost ridiculous compared to the power of Sonia's submachine gun.

However, it was enough.

There was a gasp and, if there was light. Max could have seen a stain of blood spread rapidly, tragically, down Sonia's left shoulder. Blood was soaking her dress down her chest almost to her stomach.

Stuck against the wall, Max advanced enough to hear Sonia's gasps, who was struggling uselessly to pick up the weapon that had slipped from her hands.

Already used to that light, Max, jumping over the stretched legs of Otto who had lost consciousness, ran towards Sonia.

"Quiet!

The order came sharp, hard, from Max's lips. He had arrived next to Sonia and put his foot on the butt of the submachine gun, at the same time that he projected the light of his flashlight towards the woman's eyes.

It seemed to suddenly collapse and stopped struggling to retrieve the submachine gun.

Max could have sworn that a sob came from Sonia's throat. However, he was quite skeptical about Sonia being able or capable of crying. He ignored the slightest attention and hit Sonia's wrist with the toe of his shoe. She remained motionless, closing her eyes to free her eyes from the torture of that fixed light.

Max sighed.

"I am glad that you understand that it is useless to look for a way out," he said. I would hate to have to kill you, Sonia.

"Shoot," the woman said hoarsely.

Max laughed quietly.

"It's curious. You already asked me once, a few hours ago. Anyone would say that you are a clairvoyant ... I don't know if you understand me: I mean that you can indeed die at my hands.

Sonia did not reply. She continued to avoid the light, making Max lose the sight of staring into her very black eyes, which stung furiously.

"We know that two men were with you, Sonia" said Max. Where are they?

Be quiet.

"Does this tunnel have an exit?" Asked Max.

Sonia did not answer the question. In turn, he inquired:

"How did you discover this house?

"A woman. It is true that women always play an important role in history. But I want to remind you that I ask, Sonia. And I hope this time you don't answer with lies. Where are the two men who accompanied you?

"I do not know.

Max gritted his teeth. I would like to have the courage to hit a woman. He had to get it together, even if this woman was injured and the blood formed a shiny clot on the bust of that black dress.

That desire seemed to be transmitted simultaneously from the brain to the nerves of Max, who, brutally, struck with the barrel of the gun on the woman's face, causing her to cry out in pain.

"Where are they. Sonia? Where did they come from? He inquired.

Sonia was about to lose consciousness. She would have gladly burst into sobs, to better bear that latent pain in her left shoulder. He had two bullets almost close together, relentlessly biting into his flesh.

"The tunnel ... has an exit ..." he gasped. Right now, my back is plugging her.

"Agree. But I have asked something else.

"Yes...

She seemed to faint, but was awakened by a new blow, which burst those red, luscious lips, which, in other circumstances, Max would have wanted next to his. Max, and anyone.

"Sonia.

The woman shook her head. Mists Pain. Anguish.

"Did you discover the envelope?" He inquired.

"Good sham," growled Max. Yes, we found it. And that? Naturally, we suspect that Yfremov gave the instructions verbally. Is it possible that they are taking place tonight?

Sonia slowly nodded her head. Then he said:

"Yes this night. It doesn't matter anymore that I say it. It is useless that you try to neutralize our action ...

Max narrowed his eyes. The hand holding the flashlight wavered slightly.

"Maybe not, Sonia" he said coldly. Are those two men out to sabotage new shipments of steel? What are the ships that must carry the cargo? You know all that and I'm going to know it too.

Max was surprised by the woman's reaction. He just giggled hysterically and then unexpectedly his head hung to the right side. He froze, breathing very weakly. Max's fists clenched frantically around the flashlight and pistol he held.

Still not very convinced that Sonia's swoon was legitimate, he struck a new blow against the woman's face. Only a slight moan left Sonia's throat and she collapsed to the ground, exposing the opening of the tunnel.

However, Max, in those moments, considered that there were more urgent things.

He left Sonia and ran for the stairs that led to the trap room. She heard Gretel sigh of relief, who was kneeling on the ground, watching what might happen in that gloomy tunnel.

Before Gretel could open her mouth, Max Lijo:

"Look for anything that can be used to disinfect and bandage wounds.

"Max, what? ...

Gretel broke off. Max wasn't listening. The German had disappeared again, heading towards Otto. Anxiously, he leaned over the stink; he put his ear to Otto's bloody chest and seemed relieved to catch the faint beating of a large heart.

He gathered the two lanterns, letting them both shine their light on Otto, illuminating him clearly enough.

"Otto ...

Gentle slaps on the man's cold cheeks.

Thick beads of sweat on Max's forehead.

"Otto ...!

Max shook the wounded man, whose eyes widened, casting a stupid, veiled look around him,

"Bitch ... bitch ..." Otto whispered hoarsely.

"Calm down" Max muttered ".. We can do something for you. Do not move; do not speak.

Gretel's footsteps could be heard coming alongside Max and the wounded man. Ashore he left an emergency kit and a bottle of French brandy. Apparently, the Russians also appreciated liquors that were not theirs and had nothing to do with vodka.

Max took the bottle and inserted the neck between Otto's lips.

He swallowed a few swish, feeling a surge of heat, of life. Too bad it was artificial ... But ... what the hell was Max's barbarian doing?

He had simply taken off his jacket and was trying to do the same with Otto's shirt, which was soaked in blood. When the German's torso was bare, Max took the medicine cabinet.

Without Otto's lips parting, Max did his best to stop the bleeding caused by two dangerous bullets. One of them, on the right side of the chest, under the nipple on the same side; the other, less than an inch away from the previous one.

"Easy, Otto" muttered Max "You will get out of this.

Lied.

He was lying piously.

Those two sinkers were deadly.

Otto knew very well what it was that was probing terribly painful in his chest and laughed briefly.

"Nonsense, Max ..." he said. I do not get out of this. But I hardly care. Really. I just feel like ...

It was interrupted.

The image of the bodies of Max and Gretel joined clearly came to his brain. Love. Maybe despair. What did it matter how he mastered this? Otto envied him. That vision of twenty minutes before stunned him, made him want something frantically. Something: love. The Polish girl ... How far she was ...!

"Max ...

"That?

Otto laughed again. Or was he crying?

"Is it... is it worth it for a man to die like this... for nothing? For nothing, Max! "The big man almost sobbed". All this is useless, barbarous, meaningless ... My farm ... I would be happy there, Max. You know it...

"For God's sake, shut up, Otto," Max whispered livid.

"I am very afraid. Very scared, Max ... "- Otto stammered.

Max Kroplein felt a chill. He looked away from Otto's face and looked at Gretel, who was silent, perhaps taking the same opinion as Otto.

"We'll move you upstairs, Otto" Max muttered. We will try to find some way to save you. You have to help us.

"Yes ... yes, Max ...

At that moment a muffled moan sounded from the corner where Sonia lay.

Max's and Gretel's gazes were fixed on the confused shape of the Russian's body, moving weakly.

"Take care of her, Gretel," Max muttered. " I'll try to move Otto upstairs.

When he approached Otto to grab him, the wounded man seemed to shy away from the contact. He pressed his sweaty back to the wall.

"No ... don't bother, Max ... It's useless. Thank you for having wanted to deceive me, but I know the truth very well ... Why is it that a man always knows when to die?

"Don't talk like that, Otto ...

"I repeat that I thank you, Max ... But, it is useless ... I told you before that ..., that I only regret not being able to return to my farm ... That girl, the Polish one, loves me ... I'm sure, Max. She ... she knows that I am not her enemy ... She knows how to distinguish, since currently half the world believes that the Germans are her enemies ... Why, Max? Because?

"Forget that now, Otto. We are going to...

"I won't be able to resist that move, Max ... Let me ...

Max, stunned, looked at Otto. He stared at him in disbelief and realized that Otto was right. Any effort to improve the situation of that great and clean German was useless.

"Otto, I ...

It was interrupted.

Otto's head was leaning unconsciously against the tunnel wall. He had lost consciousness again.

7

He has come to himself.

Max approached Gretel, who was kneeling next to Sonia. He gently pushed her away, taking the young woman's place. He stretched out his right hand, taking Sonia's trembling chin.

"I have deduced from all this that two men have set out to sabotage the ships with cargo of steel destined for Germany. Those ships, surely, are about to sail, so it is certain that their respective crews are on board. It is enough that you speak so that many lives of neutral people are saved, Sonia. I would like you to understand this well: neutral people. Those lives don't have to be cut short.

"The boats would also be saved" said Sonia.

Max closed his eyes briefly.

"Does it matter that much?" He inquired.

Sonia's eyes flashed. Her erect bust shook, turne, wet with blood.

"For us, yes," he said, harshly.

Max bowed his head.

Hadn't he seen, with his own eyes, helpless, almost crying with rage, what the SS and the Gestapo in close collaboration had done with the captured Russians? Women and children included. Wasn't that maddening?

Maddening...

What was it that shone in Sonia Yourskof's pupils? Wasn't it madness?

"I repeat that these are neutral people," said Max.

"Steel is for Germany" Sonia insisted.

"Despite that, Sonia.

The woman took a deep breath, which caused her to cough.

"It's okay. Maybe you are right". Anyway, I don't think there is already a solution.

"What do you mean?" Asked Max.

59

"It has been more than an hour, almost an hour and a half, that the men left in the direction of the port of the city," explained Sonia- ". The charges, quite possibly, are already in place ...

* * *

"Do you see something, Kuibshef?

"No" growled the aforementioned.

Lubyen squinted up, trying to catch the signals waiting from Stockholm harbor; They had been in the water for a long time, more than forty-five minutes, and the wait was beginning to unsettle the nerves of the Russians, totally invisible in the dark, offshore the harbor.

"I don't like Vorostok!" Said Lubyen. " You take things too easy; as if none of this was with us ...

He stopped suddenly.

There, in the distance, a reddish light shone. Half a minute later, the light was shining at a point a short distance from the first. They waited yet another half minute, and it flashed for the third time.

"Three ships," Kuibshef growled. Things get more complicated every day.

"Don't waste your time talking," grumbled the other.

They began to bring the boat closer to the docks without losing sight of the situations marked by the signalman. They saw confusedly, like great dark monsters, those heavy ships that contained their precious cargo.

Silhouettes that became more defined as they approached, until the convoy made up of three ships was something almost clear in the eyes of the two Soviets, who had already decided to abandon the inflatable boat.

They were quite close to the port and already knew the depth of those muddy bottom waters.

Lubyen slipped into the water carrying his share of the explosive charge. Meanwhile, Kuibshef sank the boat, floating an invisible buoy from the port.

The two men swam toward the ships, making no splash. It is true that his precautions were almost unnecessary, since the crew of the merchant ships did not usually worry about what happened in the waters of the port.

A little later, they disappeared from the surface after crossing a sign.

Both searched the hulls of the ships, trying to place their delayed-explosion magnetic charges in the most vulnerable points of the ship.

The charges, of the «lamprey» type, were distributed according to the experience that those two men already possessed, who could be compared to strange sea monsters, although with their hands frozen with cold and their lungs on the verge of exploding.

Every now and then, a face bruised from the cold would surface. An eager breath of air was enough to send the man back in search of the next point where he should place the load.

The operation was carried out quickly, but without nerves, calmly,.

The first to swim to where the boat was sunk was Lubyen, who located the buoy. It was easy to sink and recover the boat, when the other one arrived.

They quietly took up their posts and began their return to their headquarters.

Once more they looked at those silhouettes, already blurred, that would soon explode. Each "lamprey" explosion would follow, a shudder of the ship in question, and a cloud of water would jump violently.

As always. Then the ship, seriously damaged, would sink with its load of steel.

* * *

Max Kropelin clenched his fists. Mentally he followed the movements of those men and imagined what was going to happen.

"What ships are those, Sonia?" He asked. Do you know their names?

"No.

"Think it over," said Max, smiling coldly.

A flash of fear passed through the Russian's taste buds. Max guessed that he really did not know the data, so it was going to be almost impossible to prevent the explosions or, at the very least, for the crews to abandon the ship.

"Okay," Max sighed. I hope this is your last operation. Who is in charge of your group?

"I" said Sonia.

"Do you have any other men besides those two?

Be quiet.

Max shook his head.

"I am willing to destroy you," he said. Your network of sabotage must disappear. They may send other agents, but I assure you it will not be easy for them to organize. I know that you have been here since before the war started. The Russians did not fall asleep, but keep in mind that the rest of us are starting to wake up now.

A sneer of contempt touched the Russian's lips.

"Don't strain. I won't say anything else. We will see what you are capable of doing with me "he said.

"At least you will see what I intend to do with the two who have to arrive at any moment" said Max, smiling harshly. As for you, we will find a solution. I'm not a murderer ... I haven't been until now.

Gretel looked at Max a little scared. The young German could not hide her concern; the stay in that tunnel drowned her.

"Max ... let's go upstairs" he said. Otto won't last long here.

"It's okay. Let's go.

He got closer to Sonia, forcing her to sit up. Then he pushed her forward. The woman did not resist and began to walk under the threat of the pistol that Max had given to Gretel.

Max then walked over to Otto and put the neck of the French brandy bottle between his pale lips. Otto seemed to revive himself.

"We'll get out of here, Otto-" growled Max- ". Get up and lean on me, Otto gave a broken laugh.

"Stand up? I have them destroyed ... Look at them, Max.

Max shone the flashlight at Otto's feet and paled horribly when he saw what had happened. The right foot was smashed, undone. He could never use it ... assuming he survived his chest wounds, which Max doubted.

However, Max reacted. Said:

"Agree. I'll carry you on my back, Otto didn't protest. She was going to hold on to any chance of saving herself no matter how weak.

She felt Max's shoulder on her stomach and then swayed, as Max swayed slightly, under Otto's weight.

Max made a sign and Gretel forced Sonia to walk forward. When they reached the stairs, the first to climb was Gretel. Once upstairs, she forced Sonia, who had preceded her, to stand in a corner of the room, away from the door. For her part, Gretel waited for Max, helping him move Otto.

He was carefully placed on the ground, with his back against the wall.

Once the operation was over, Max walked slowly towards Sonia, who remained standing, livid, biting her lips to keep from crying out in pain.

"You've had time to think, Sonia" said Max.

"Will you release me if I speak?" The woman inquired.

"Try it" Max smiled crookedly.

At that moment there was a noise at the door of the house and Max, reacting quickly, jumped on Sonia, gagging her with his right hand before the woman could scream.

Max crushed the woman with the weight of his body and gestured to Gretel, who leaned against the wall by the front door of that room.

The door had been opened and the hall light came on, leaving a man perfectly visible, who began to walk towards Sonia's room.

Max giggled silently and looked at the back of Sonia's neck. It would take a single hit to get rid of her for a while. He dropped his left hand, edge-on, on the back of his neck, and he noticed that Sonia's body relaxed. He put it down and drew his pistol.

He walked noiselessly to the door and whispered:

"Don't move, Gretel.

He left that room and followed that man, who had also turned on the light in Sonia's room and was looking, puzzled, around him.

"Don't turn around," ordered Max's voice dryly.

The man's body jerked sharply, but he obeyed. He froze, turning his back on Max, who was advancing on him. The first thing Max did was slide his left hand down the Russian's chest, finding a pistol under his left armpit.

He threw it under Sonia's bed, and said:

"That's better.

"Where is Sonia?" Asked the guy.

"Now sleep. You have a job. Let's go.

He made him turn around and then pushed him into the trap room, where the phone was located. With the light coming from the lobby, it was enough to see the disk of the device, and Max ordered:

"Call the port offices and indicate the name of the ships that are in danger of being blown up.

The Russian blinked.

He took a look around him and discovered Sonia motionless on the ground, Otto, who was looking at him with veiled eyes, and the silent Gretel, whose right hand also held a pistol.

"I won't do any of that," the man growled.

Max slammed the barrel of the pistol into the Russian's left ear, who screeched and staggered.

The cry of that man accelerated the recovery of Sonia, who shuddered and opened her eyes, she bit her lips when she saw her compatriot and murmured:

"Vorostok ... Idiot.

Vorostok looked at her helplessly.

"I've been calling you on the phone" he said- "Since you weren't answering, I decided to find out what was happening.

"You could take precautions," Sonia said dryly.

"I'm not as smart as you are," said the Russian.

"Enough. I will shoot to kill if within five seconds you have not communicated with the port offices "Max intervened, planting himself before Vorostok, staring at him.

The satin looked away to fix it on Sonia. Said:

"I'm not too brave either, Sonia.

The woman shrugged her shoulders. He bent his head to hide the gleam in his eyes. Vorostok was certainly not a smart man. But he was lying about his value. This meant that there was some chance of turning the tide of the situation. Vorostok would do something ...

The Russian, closely watched by Max, took the phone, and reached out with his right hand as if to dial the corresponding number.

What he actually did was slam the handset against Max's armed hand.

The blow worked and Max, surprised, was forced to deflect the weapon from Vorostok's body. His immediate reaction was to hit Max's stomach with his left fist and then a blow with his right elbow in the face, which made Max take several steps back, until he tripped over the trip tended by Sonia, who reached out with both hands towards him. the pistol that the German was holding loosely.

Sonia took the pistol, but already Gretel, who had come out of her stupor, was shooting at her, missing, but giving Max time to rebuild and prevent Sonia from firing in turn.

Gretel's second shot was aimed at Vorostok's body: it vibrated, but the bullet could not contain the Russian's leap towards the window from which the sea could be seen.

Vorostok broke the glass, shielding his face with his hands and arms, but his body did not get through the window frame.

The second bullet fired by Gretel at Vorostok was much better targeted, digging into the center of his back.

His strength suddenly lost, his momentum cut off, Vorostok slumped against the edges of the broken glass. A cry of pain echoed through the room; a scream that was cut off abruptly, and Vorostok fell backward to the ground, showing his bloody chest, with several small ridges embedded in it. His eyes wore an expression of madness already frozen by death.

Gretel, deathly pale, her right hand hanging limp by her side, gazed, hypnotized, at that body covered in blood.

Meanwhile, Max had completely dominated Sonia, recovering his weapon.

"Damn assassin!" Growled Max, "A lot of people are going to die, Sonia. People who don't have to die.

"Nothing can be helped anymore," said Sonia. Vorostok was the only one who knew the names of those ships. On the other hand, even if he had communicated with the port offices, they would not have achieved anything either. Charges will explode at any moment.

"Which means those two men will be showing up here soon. They must be coming- "Max muttered.

Sonia did not reply.

He was breathing sourly, and in his eyes you could see the gleam produced by fever from his wounds, which did not stop flowing with blood.

"The medicine cabinet, Gretel," Max muttered.

"No ..., don't worry so much about me," Sonia said hoarsely. I won't be able to thank you.

But Gretel was already coming down the stairs of the trap, looking for the medicine cabinet. She returned shortly after and it was she herself who leaned next to Sonia, tearing her dress, to reveal a white, round, warm shoulder.

Max walked away from there and headed toward the trap, closing it. He was not in the least concerned about the arrival of the two rank-and-file saboteurs, since as soon as they opened the trap they would find themselves facing the barrel of his pistol.

Then Max approached Otto.

"Hey, Max ... I've been trying to grab the bottle for a long time," Otto muttered.

Max, without saying a word, handed the other the brandy bottle.

Otto took a drink and tears came to his eyes.

"Give me a gun, Max," he said later. Ill try to help you.

"No need, Otto," growled Max.

"Give me a gun ...!" The man exploded hysterically, grabbing Max by the lapels of his light jacket, dirty with mud and splattered with blood.

Max, calmly, detached himself from Otto's hands.

"Calm down, Otto," he said. I am enough alone.

Otto narrowed his eyes. His face was shiny with sweat.

"You guessed what I think, huh?" He grumbled.

Max stared at him silently.

"You have to understand, Max," the man muttered. " I can't take these pains anymore ... "Give me a gun ... Or the bottle. Do something, Max ... Can't you hear me?

Max bowed his head.

"I can't access that, Otto," he muttered.

"Then get me out of here.

"Two men are still missing. We can't leave now, you understand? If we leave them alive, everything will have been useless ... Even your sacrifice, Otto.

"My sacrifice ... What the hell does anything matter to me? I didn't want war, Max ... Why should I die? I want to go back to Germany ... I shouldn't have left there ... I shouldn't have left ...

Max handed the bottle to Otto, and said:

"Drink up, Otto.

"Well ... You're thinking that I'm a coward, that I can't bear the pain, huh, Max?"

"Do not say foolishness.

"Do you think me brave?

"That doesn't matter now, Otto.

"Unclear...

Otto drank again. Only the alcohol, which burned his stomach, was able to mitigate the intense pain caused by his wounds.

Then, his eyes, somewhat veiled, settled on Sonia, who resisted, biting her lips, the healing of her wounds. She, the cursed one, had killed him.

"What are you going to do with that woman, Max?" He inquired, without taking his eyes off Sonia's bare shoulder.

"I do not know...

"I do," Otto cut in.

Max took a deep breath. He knew very well what Otto was thinking at the moment. Naturally, it would have been very comfortable for him to let Otto kill the Russian. Still, Max held himself responsible for what might happen, and he disliked the idea of letting Otto coldly murder the woman.

True, it would solve a problem for him, but ... Why the hell does the worst always happen?

"I don't think you'll feel satisfied after killing Sonia, Otto-" Max muttered at last. " That was what you thought, right?

Otto drank again. He leaned his back against the wall.

"It's true," he mused. You know I'm starting to feel a lot better, Max?

Max looked at the bottle.

"I celebrate it," he murmured.

"What do you plan to do now?" Otto inquired.

"Expect. I already told you.

"And later?

Max was surprised by the question.

"Later? -" he growled. I do not know. I have not decided anything,

"Are you going back to Germany?

"It is not that easy, Otto.

"Sure ... It's not easy. I have never felt so much desire to return as at this time, Max "said Otto." I think I would do some things differently.

"Do you regret something?

Otto smiled, which twitched, turning into my wince.

"I regret what I haven't done, Max" he said. I suppose something like this must be felt by all dying people. One gets the impression that he has stupidly wasted his life

A trickle of blood trickled down the left corner of Otto's mouth. Max hoarsely said:

"Speak no more. Otto. Rest well.

<h1 style="text-align:center">8</h1>

The rubber dinghy silently stuck to the rocky cliff face. With a strong wire it was secured to the ledge of a rock and the two men dedicated their effort to run the rock that covered the entrance of the tunnel from the outside.

When they succeeded, Lubyen slipped through the opening, then aiding Kuibshef. Once the two men were inside the tunnel, they hoisted the boat, pulling the wire. They deflated it by moving it inside.

The opening was closed and Lubyen reached for a natural ledge, where the lantern was left for such cases.

He didn't touch her off the shelf; he simply pressed the switch, and the light hit the spot where the Soviet agents had left their clothes.

The two men stripped off their rubber suits, wearing normal clothes.

"I smell like gunpowder, Lubyen," Kuibshef growled.

"Silly stuff.

"I have a very fine nose.

Lubyen ignored it.

"Are you ready?" He growled,

"Yes.

Lubyen took the flashlight and headed down the tunnel, heading for the stairs.

Kuibshef felt strangely uneasy. It smelled of gunpowder. Of course Lubyen was much smarter than he, but when it came to appreciating danger Kuibshef had a highly developed instinct. It was not the first time that his life had come into play.

Lubyen was apparently thinking of other things. He ascended the stairs and pushed the trap with his left hand. He poked his head out

He saw, very fleetingly, like a flash of lightning that enclosed death, that the darkness was truncated, violently, savagely.

Fleeting. Very fleeting.

Lubyen didn't even know that his scream was hideous. A short, broken cry.

With two bullets to his head, Lubyen let the trap close again and rolled down the stairs, dropping the flashlight and running over Kuibshef.

The two men were left on the damp ground. Kuibshef, shaking off the weight of Lubyen's corpse, took the lantern and stepped back toward the opening in the cliff without doubting for a single moment that his companion was dead. He had briefly seen Lubyen's shattered forehead.

Feeling that the anguish, the terror, formed a lump in his throat. Kuibshef backed up to the end of the tunnel, and tried moving the solid rock.

It was useless. It took two strong men to move it.

Thick beads of sweat began to trickle down the face of that man, who was looking desperately around, searching for a way out that did not exist. Open the trap and have his head blown off like Lubyen?

"No, no ..." - he murmured hoarsely.

However, he started walking back towards the stairs. He felt cornered, sunk. What could have happened?

* * *

While Otto, almost drunk, was laughing silently when the trap was closed again, Gretel on the verge of fainting, looked at Max in astonishment.

He had fired twice without warning without waiting for anything. He had killed with pleasure to do so. It was read in his eyes in those moments. Death was seen in Max's blue-gray pupils.

"Max ..." Gretel whispered, like a reproach.

Max narrowed his eyes.

"So far, one has died," he said. Only one, Gretel. I cannot forgive those men nor do I care how they look. What's more, I just had an idea. Come closer.

Gretel, stunned, obeyed.

Again she believed, in those moments, that Max was a stranger to her. Max's face was very pale, contorted. It was clear in his pupils that he was not lying, that he was determined to kill, whatever it was.

Max looked into Gretel's eyes without his expression softening. Dryly, I order:

"Bring the clothes from Sonia's bed. Pre-moistened.

"Max ... I don't understand ...

"You'll understand right away-" Max cut in abruptly. I cannot forget that dozens of men may die tonight, in a few minutes. Dozens of men ... You don't understand that either? I've seen it too long, Gretel. Too much time. And not just men. I have seen dozens die, hundreds, women and children for whom war was cruel, incomprehensible. I can't tolerate it! The mass murderers, those cruel, blind swords, must disappear. It doesn't matter whether they are Nazis or Russians. They must die. Really, the war has to serve something: so that the worst dies. Unfortunately, this is not always the case. But it will happen sometime. We will ever be free from murderers. The clothes on Sonia's bed, wet! "Max shouted.

Gretel's mouth widened, as if she was struggling to breathe.

He did not make a single comment. Almost running, trying to hide his fear, his sobs, he ran towards Sonia's room.

The Russian, for her part, looked at Max as if he were a strange phenomenon of nature. At that time, the Russian felt real panic, thinking that if Max did not regain his usual serenity she was going to have a bad time.

Otto was still laughing.

He looked at Sonia, burning that white and naked shoulder with his veiled pupils. He really had been stupid. Life has very good things that he had overlooked, even once he had fallen in love he was clumsily choosing to fight.

Absurd

What he had to do was go anywhere with the Pole, marry her, and be happy. Damn stupid! Damn blindness!

He chose the Nazi party because he had not yet experienced its horrors. He was proud when he donned the 'Wehrmacht' uniform and was posted to a 'Panzer' division, just like Max. It was there that they met and began the fight with enthusiasm.

Then everything changed.

The nobility of the army was wallowed, muddied by the rearguard groups, by those murderous SS commandos

Otto closed his eyes and stopped laughing.

He needed another drink.

He understood that it was not very dignified to die drunk, but he did not feel up to anything else. For him, dignity had been lost long before; everyone had lost her.

Finally, Gretel arrived, with a pile of discreetly damp clothes. He left her, silently, at Max's feet.

"What are you going to do, Max?" He inquired.

"Can't you imagine?" Max smiled coldly.

"Me...

"That man is in there half scared to death," Max said. At least I would be. After all, all I'll do is convince him that it's better to die sooner.

That said, Max stopped paying attention to Gretel, and leaned toward the bundle of wet clothing. He set fire to the end of a sheet and waited until the smoke was almost unbearable in that room.

It was then that Max opened the trap, and with his foot sent the smoking pyre down the stairs, closing quickly.

Coughing, he looked at Gretel and said:

"Open the window wide, Gretel.

The woman started toward the window, through the smoke, avoiding Vorostok's corpse.

Apparently the broken glass did not produce enough ventilation for the smoke to escape.

Gretel opened the window and stood by her for a moment, breathing in the outside air at the top of her lungs.

Then he looked at Max.

He remained alert, standing before the trap, motionless, knowing what had to come.

* * *

Naturally, the smoke was not visible in the darkness of the tunnel, especially considering that Kuibshef, as a further precaution, had turned off the flashlight.

However, he began to cough.

He began to notice a painful irritation in his eyes. Then the unmistakable smell. He did indeed have a very fine nose and an exact sense of danger.

"Damn ...!" He muttered.

He understood immediately: either he would come out of there, ready to take two bullets to the head, or he would die asphyxiated. Given the choice, anyone would opt for the first death. A quick, almost sweet death.

He switched on the flashlight and took a submachine gun from the small arsenal, which he placed under his right arm, index finger glued to the trigger, and advanced towards the stairs.

He tried to stomp on the pile of burned clothes, but only succeeded in increasing the smoke,

Not even daring to breathe, he started up the stairs.

As a first act, what he did was pull the trigger of the submachine gun, firing a blast of lead that splintered the trap, lifting it slightly due to the impacts.

He fired again, then quickly, with the same barrel of the submachine gun, pushed the wood, which opened wide, allowing Kuibshef to inhale a blast of almost pure air.

Just one.

As his lungs were filling with air, what he had feared came. There, before his red, irritated, watery eyes, death unleashed.

Max Kropelin, immutable, his pistol held tight, fired several times.

The flashes erupted into a single fiery tongue. The lead parted, malignant, deadly, towards Kuibshef's face.

In a few seconds, that face disappeared from Max's view, although he could see some bone particles jump.

Once the corpse bounced down the stairs, Max hastily closed the trap again, preventing the smoke from filling that room again.

Then, staring at the wooden rectangle, he remained motionless for a moment.

"Max."

He did not turn.

"Let's get out of here, Max.

Gretel's voice was pleading, somewhat high-pitched, as if the young woman were on the verge of hysteria.

Finally, Max turned and faced Gretel. The girl's eyes were full of tears. He bit his lip. Perhaps everything that had happened had been too much for a simple woman, who the most she had done was to steal some documents from the immense Nazi archive.

"Yes ..." Max whispered. Let's go from here.

It was then that they both perceived a muffled moan, which expressed indescribable anguish.

9

Otto began to slide in the direction of the woman, who seemed to have fainted. Maybe the smoke; perhaps the pain of his wounds on that shoulder that was an obsession for the German.

In those tense moments, neither Max nor Gretel had noticed Otto, who was advancing slowly but surely. The French brandy had to be of something. Dammit...! Otto knew that the generals, politicians and fat people of the Nazi party made themselves take brandy from occupied France, as well as "champagne" and some typical French products.

Good cognac, yes. Those damned knew what they were doing.

Otto coughed and noticed that it was becoming more and more difficult for him to breathe. But he did not attach importance to it. I was only asking for a few more minutes of life.

He laughed strangely, thinking that at least he would have done something that he would not regret leaving pending.

He looked back at Sonia, who was still with her eyes closed. Very pale. It showed his white throat; a throbbing throat that grew larger before Otto's reddened eyes.

When he reached the woman, Otto looked at Max and Gretel, who were not paying him the slightest attention. That Gretel, according to Otto, had eyes only for Max. Better. Best for Max; a lucky guy.

It was then that the shots began to sound.

Otto didn't wait any longer. He advanced both hands, cold, stiff, and surrounded Sonia's throat.

The woman, at the contact, also due to the explosion of the shots, opened her eyes and, horrified, tried to scream.

He could no longer do it.

"Die, bitch ..., die ..." Otto stammered, "People like you don't deserve to live ..., they don't deserve to breathe ...

Sonia tried to argue, but her strength failed her. Those fingers around her throat seized her nerves, darkened her brain.

"Max had forgotten about you ..." Otto panted. I do not. You are the main culprit of all this. You are the worst murderer. What do you care if innocent people die ...? What do you care ...? You've never seen it, have you? I do. I have seen it...!

Otto, with his face flushed, with the veins in his temples on the verge of exploding, was half upright, gathering his already scant strength to squeeze Sonia's neck.

The woman had stopped struggling and her face was turning dark.

Moaned. I was just moaning.

"Drop her, Otto ... Come on, drop her ...!

Nor did he hear anything.

The German giant noted a strange pleasure in sticking his thumbs in Sonia's jugular. Still, he offered no slightest resistance when Max's hands managed to separate his from that brutally severed neck.

When Max leaned down to examine Sonia more closely, he sighed and said:

"You have strangled her, Otto.

Otto did not reply.

Really, the effects of that half-drunkenness were wearing off and Max's words bounced off his bloated, exhausted brain.

He shrugged and stammered:

"He... deserved it, Max... didn't he?

"Surely, Otto. But it happens that ... Good. Silly stuff. I was going to say that it is a woman.

"It was... it was a monster, huh, Max?

Max stared at Otto. He discovered anxiety in the man's veiled pupils. Otto almost certainly expected Max to confirm that Sonia had been a monster. Otto waited for that confirmation as a mitigating factor to ease his conscience.

"It was, Otto," he said. Now, she's just a dead woman. One more. It hardly matters; Do you understand

Otto nodded awkwardly and said:

Thank you, Max.

"Bah. Now, we will get out of here. We will return to the city. Maybe some doctor will save you, Otto. Let's go?

"Yes Yes. I would spend saving myself, Max. We've done a good job, huh? Very good. Of course, really, you have been the one who has carried the weight of the work, but I also consider myself satisfied. A great triumph, Max.

Max licked his lips.

I was going to say that this was not a triumph, but quite the opposite: a resounding failure.

"Yes ... a great triumph, Otto" he whispered. We have dismantled a dangerous Soviet sabotage network. A great triumph ...

He turned to look at Gretel, who had approached them both. Gretel noticed that Max's pupils had softened. He even found that man who had recently shot, mad with rage, relaxed at some murderers.

Come on, Gretel. Help me carry Otto. We will take you to the car.

"Yes, Max,

Again, Max carried Otto's weight and began to walk towards the exit of that house, which was a large grave. It was Gretel who opened the door to the outside, and air filled Max's lungs, in whose mind the sight of Lubyen's shattered forehead and Kuibshef's shattered face still danced.

However, he noted that he did not feel the slightest remorse. After all, those two men deserved death.

They finally reached the car, parked behind a clump of trees just off the road. Gretel slipped into the vehicle, taking the front seat behind the wheel.

There the girl felt much better. Especially since he had left behind that horror of the dead.

Otto was ushered into the back seats and Max took up position beside him.

"-Get up, Gretel," Max muttered.

The young woman backed up, backing up until she had a turning angle. Then he turned onto the highway in the direction of Stockholm, whose buildings, dark masses dotted with light, were visible from a relative distance.

Gretel turned slightly and inquired:

"Where to, Max?

Max was thoughtful for a moment.

An idea crept into his brain, though he dismissed it as useless. It was disheartening to know that there was nothing they could do for the ships on whose hulls the evil explosive "lampreys" were stuck. However, he said:

"To the port, Gretel.

Otto shuddered.

"To port, Max?" He asked weakly.

"Why not?

"We're wasting time ... And I'm bleeding to death, Max ..." Otto gasped. " I want to live, you understand? I want to live...

Those words, the effort of uttering them, seemed to exhaust his strength and Otto lay on the seat, breathing weakly and with his eyes closed.

Max gritted his teeth. It was clear that the minutes of Otto's life were numbered.

A multitude of thoughts raced through Max's brain; multitude of memories. It seemed as if his life had started a year earlier; He was only able to remember what happened in that year; in what had given his life a tragic, unexpected turn.

Mentally, to cheer himself up a bit, he thought that he had been lucky after all. Otto no. Ni Kurbjuhn; nor others like them. He preserved life and ...

Max fixed his eyes on Gretel's hair; that dark brown that shone like a glimmer of hope.

And Gretel, yes.

In those moments, Max wished it was all over; He wanted to give up the fight and find another place to live with Gretel. That city, Stockholm, would soon grow close to his anti-Nazi action group.

The car had already driven into the city, almost paralyzed at this time of night.

Some lights flashed by.

"Maybe with the car we will attract attention in the port, and more at this time, Gretel" said Max ", Park as close as possible. As we cannot carry with Otto, we will leave him here until our return,

Otto stirred.

"No ... don't delay, Max ..." he muttered weakly.

"No man.

"I would not like ... to die alone ... here, do you understand?

Max closed his eyes briefly.

"Nobody talks about dying, Otto.

"I ... I know very well what I feel. No one can fool me anymore ... Not even myself "whispered the German.

There was silence inside the car. Max looked at Gretel and noted the tension that the woman was enduring. What he could not see were the tears that ran down the livid female cheeks.

Soon after, Gretel was braking on a street next to the harbor, about a hundred yards away.

Silently the girl got out and waited for Max to do so.

Gretel avoided looking into the car. Her gaze was fixed on the few lights of the port, shrouded in mist, as if the tragedy that was guessed had her hypnotized.

"Until now, Otto," Max muttered. I wish I could still do something for those ships .... Otto,

Be quiet.

Otto was not moving. He didn't seem to have heard Max. He no longer seemed to hear anything from this world.

Suddenly distraught, sweaty, Max leaned over, examining his companion's closed eyes. He lowered the lower eyelid of one eye, without Otto moving,

"Otto ...

It was an icy, muffled whisper.

"Dead ... But what are you surprised at, Max? "Wondered the German." You were waiting for it, and now ...

He felt a lump in his throat.

When he reacted, thinking of Gretel, who was waiting outside, he tried to calm his expression.

Slowly, he left the vehicle and approached the young woman.

"Come on, Gretel," he murmured.

They walked quickly, nervously, in the direction of the port. They had not yet "walked twenty steps, when muffled, drowned, the first explosion rang out. The bodies of the two Germans vibrated. Anguished, they quickened their pace.

The second. Third.

They could already see the water leap, pushed upward by a savage, brutal hand. More explosions. The cries of the few people on the docks began to be audible. The alarm rang.

Panting, Max and Gretel arrived in front of the harbor and stared in amazement at the monstrous scene. One of the ships already had the stern almost sunk and the fever of its crew members was noticed, who hastily lowered the boats, amid great confusion.

From the other side of the ships, almost simultaneously with the explosion of a "lamprey" placed under the fuel tanks, a terrifying red-black flare shot up into the sky, and the ship began to make water rapidly.

Meanwhile, in the port, alarm sirens sounded, which turned all that into something hallucinatory.

"Let's go, Max ... Let's go!" Gretel almost sobbed. We can't do anything here. Nothing can be avoided anymore.

Max, still stunned, nodded.

"Yes Yes. Let's go.

He grabbed her by the arm and dragged her in the direction of the rental car stopped at the corner.

"I can never forget this, Max," Gretel whispered.

Max smiled bitterly. Indeed, there are things that can never be forgotten. They always remain hidden, but alive, latent, in any corner of the brain. He knew very well that it was true. He also knew that many nights Gretel would jump out of bed, anguished by those explosions, by that thick blaze, by the boats that capsized terribly, while innocent men sought their salvation.

When they reached the car, Gretel took her place again and Max moved to her side. The girl looked at Max in surprise. She questioned him with her big blue eyes, somewhat misty.

"Otto is dead," Max whispered.

"My God...

That was it. It was enough. It was a heartrending plea. To hate war you have to live it up close, not with the Gestapo archives more or less close. That didn't matter. And Gretel was ill-prepared to watch people die en masse, savagely, as if they owed something to Nature.

"Gretel ...

Max's voice was muffled, soft. The girl stared at him, as if in those moments she was discovering him again.

"You must react, Gretel," Max murmured.

"I understand," the young woman whispered. What do we do now?

Max glanced quickly toward the back seats, glancing at Otto's corpse. He licked his lips and said:

"For now, we must hide Otto's body. No one should associate what happened in that house with the Germans, do you understand? Sooner or later the Swedish authorities will find her and understand a lot of things when they discover the tunnel. We will let you believe that only Russian agents have intervened in this. Anyway, it can be said that it has almost been so. And in any case, they are the culprits. We will therefore count on the Swedish police to tighten their surveillance and I do not believe that the Russians will insist on sabotaging ships in the port of Stockholm.

Gretel nodded.

"Okay, Max," he murmured, as he started the car, thinking that this was the second time that night that he had done this macabre task.

Seconds later, the vehicle disappeared from that scene.

"What will we do next, Max? I'm scared, "said Gretel.

Max took a moment to respond.

"Tell me, Gretel ... Are you still thinking about not going back to Germany for the time being?"

"Yes, Max.

"Well ... I've been thinking and I think the best thing would be to disappear from Stockholm" said the German.

Gretel looked at him in surprise.

"But this is where, currently, we could form a strong anti-Nazi group, Max," he said.

Max smiled slightly.

"I do not doubt it. But Stockholm will also be, from now on, a city to which the Gestapo will be attracted. And, where possible, we must avoid clashes with the Gestapo. The more they don't know about our organizations abroad, the better.

"Understand. Then...?

"A good place would certainly be Oslo. We will also have work there ", replied Max.

The young woman sighed.

"It will be Oslo," he said.

"Of course, we would have to find a way to let Horst know what we want," said Max. " But at the moment, I don't want to think about that. Now, I find myself ... tired.

After saying these words, Max leaned back in the seat and let the car roll, guided by Gretel's instincts. Once again he recognized that he had been lucky.

Gretel gave him a quick look, but said nothing. I was puzzled

Since when did she love Max? Maybe forever ... But at least it seemed so. Therefore. What did the rest matter? War? She just wanted peace.

The vehicle had already left the city behind and was once again serving as a hearse.

Anywhere in the open would be a good place to hide Otto's body. If they ever found out, a lot could have happened. In any case, it would be very difficult for the Swedish police to identify him.

Gretel shuddered. Really, that way of being buried was not pleasant; there was not even a grave. That was almost as much as denying that the man had ever lived.

He was surprised by Max's voice, since he believed that his eyes were still closed. Max had said:

"Stop here, Gretel.

The car came to a gentle stop.

10

The car stopped in front of the door of the establishment that rented them. Quickly, Max and Gretel got out and started walking. The detail of the car could be dangerous, since its disappearance would be reported to the police and Gretel would be searched.

"Tonight we will part ways, Gretel," Max said. I will accompany you to your hotel and I will return to my apartment. I will prepare everything for a disappearance that does not arouse suspicion, understood?

"Yes.

They seemed a little more animated. They walked very close together and it seemed that all that was already very close.

They did not seem to know that it would be dawn soon.

It took them fifteen minutes to reach the discreet hotel where Gretel was staying, Max took the young woman by the shoulders and looked her in the eyes. He noticed the weariness that dominated this girl, whose pupils were somewhat dull, and slightly bluish circles had formed under her eyes.

"I'll wait for you at the nightstand, Gretel," Max muttered.

The young woman, smiling, nodded.

"Nothing else, Max?" He inquired.

Max looked along the street, asleep.

He wrapped both arms around Gretel's waist and held her gently against him. Gretel had raised her face and her thin pink lips were parted.

Max kissed her hard and thought it was a shame to have to abandon the woman right now. Gretel must have thought something similar, since she kissed Max long, passionately.

"See you later, Max-" he whispered, when he pulled away from the man.

Max nodded.

He let the young woman head towards the entrance of the hotel. Once he was out of sight, Max began to walk to his apartment.

It was only after lighting a cigarette and blowing a thick puff of smoke into the sky that he realized that it was dawn.

For her part, Gretel slowly walked past the hotel reception desk and noticed that the sleepy eyes of the concierge on duty would perk up at the sight.

The idiot must have believed that Gretel had spent a ... restless night.

True, but not in the sense expressed by the mischievousness of the janitor's little eyes.

Anyway, Gretel didn't care. She was too tired, too stunned by everything that had happened to notice this man.

He took the elevator to the second floor and went into his room. The surprise left her frozen, immobile.

* * *

The nightstand, like every day at sunset, was lively. Generally, it was couples of young people who were looking for the cool and strategic places of that viewpoint located in front of the sea.

He felt safer that afternoon, calmer. The atmosphere of the Swedish capital is serene, peaceful, it helps people feel good.

Max looked at his wristwatch and deduced that Gretel couldn't be long in coming. He felt a real need to see her again, to feel her next to him, to kiss her. Gretel, by her presence, would indicate to him that everything that had happened the night before had nothing to do with a dream.

Max already had a good idea of what they should do the next day.

They would leave Sweden as silently as they had arrived. The combination was the railway to Mariestad, on the shores of Lake Véner. They could spend a few days there, mingling with the Swedish vacationers. A good place to go unnoticed. Then Oslo.

Max looked up, trying to see Gretel's arrival again. And he saw her.

For this reason, Max's brow furrowed first, so that his eyes, later, acquired a clear expression of surprise. Gretel no. I arrived alone.

He let the girl and her companion come to his side, and said:

"I don't understand, Horst ...

The little man with the thick glasses smiled.

Sit down, Max. And you, Gretel.

Both young men obeyed and Horst Anthelme sat down next to them. Relax, he lit a cigarette. Then he stared at Max and said:

"Gretel has explained everything that happened to me, Max. Good job; really.

"Are you here because you didn't trust me?" Max asked, tense.

"Don't be silly," Horst growled, fixing his shortsighted eyes on Max's. Things have happened in Berlin.

"Stuff?

"We have been discovered. My organization has been dismantled in the blink of an eye. Max "said Horst." I still think it is a dream that I am here right now. I don't even know how I was able to escape from the Gestapo. Naturally, my duty was to appear here and update you on the facts.

Max gritted his teeth,

"How did the Gestapo discover you?" He inquired,

Horst shrugged.

"You already know that they are very powerful. It's hard to continually outwit them. I suspect that Gretel's disappearance had something to do with it. That also means that, possibly, they will locate her and try to find out more. Understood?

Max and Gretel exchanged a look. Max licked his lips then.

"Understood, Horst," he said. Are you planning to stay in Stockholm?

Horst smiled slightly and shook his head.

"That would be foolish, Max," he replied. I'm already an old acquaintance of those damn things. On the other hand, you have finished the action work in Stockholm. It is a pity that, as a result of what happened in Berlin, it will be difficult to propagandize for our group.

"Yeah ... It's a shame," Max muttered.

Horst blinked.

"What's wrong with you?" He inquired.

"Well ..., I was thinking of Kurbjuhn and Otto. They have fallen, Horst. I don't know ... I have the impression that they died for nothing. Stupidly and uselessly.

Horst was silent for a moment.

"I think you're wrong, Mas" he said, finally, softly- ". Nobody dies for nothing. His sacrifice will open the eyes of many people; Do you understand

"And that? If only we lost the war ...!

Horst smiled.

"Don't be absurd, Max," he said. Why should we lose the war? That, at the moment, has no foundation whatsoever. The whole of Europe is dominated by our troops. Very well. We must try to help those troops from our field. For example: the elimination of the Soviet network that sabotaged Swedish steel shipments. Now, what it is about is to annul Nazism. No more Slavs. No more murder, you understand?

Max sighed.

"Sure, Horst. Perfectly, "he growled.

"Agree. We will move to Oslo

"You too?" Growled Max.

"Does it bother you?" Horst sneered.

"Well ... As much as bothering me, no. But ... I had thought of resting a little, the young man murmured.

Horst frowned. He looked out to sea thoughtfully.

"We need you, Max," he murmured at last. " Or do you think the fight is over? I'd say start, you know? The United States will launch in full force and we must spare Germany as much damage as we can.

"You always convince me, Horst" smiled wearily, Max.

"I expected it," Horst sighed.

"Already. Good evening.

Horst was a touch surprised-

"That...?

"I said good night, Horst" smiled Max "We will see you in Oslo. Does it seem bad to you?

Horst looked at Max and then at Gretel. The girl was slightly flushed and was staring very intently at the table, as if discovering at that moment that the top was made of marble.

The old man laughed,

"Devils...! I'm sorry, Max "he said". Actually, old people tend to be quite heavy. Good luck, Max, Bye, Gretel,

Horst stood up and, smiling, began to walk away, followed by the gaze of both young men. Horst was not that old. He conserved a good part of his physical energies and great mental strength. The man who had defied the Berlin Gestapo could not be just anybody.

It wasn't, actually.

When he was out of sight, between the avenue gardens, Max looked at Gretel.

"I was afraid he would come between us" said Max- ". And no. A little life has to be ours, Gretel. We have the right to,

Gretel smiled. An attractive smile, cheerful in those moments.

"Of course, Max. Let's go?

Max looked at her, surprised.

"Where to?" He inquired.

He followed the gaze of Gretel, who had settled on those cool gardens, overflowing with couples; there they talked about love, there many illusions were born.

"I'd like to walk in the gardens, Max," he said. I confess that it always seemed a very stupid thing to me and I have not had occasion to verify otherwise. Actually, in my life there have been very few flowers ...

It was interrupted. A sudden cloud had slightly clouded his eyes.

Max understood. Gretel was also one of those who had sacrificed themselves. But that had to be forgotten. After all, it had been for something ... Exactly: for something:

He remembered Horst's words: "No one dies for nothing." So it was. No one dies for anything and no one sacrifices for anything. The phrase could be used with many people. He had not yet forgotten Sonia, those three Russians who had fought ...

"Come on, Gretel," he said, suddenly interrupting her thoughts. Life had to be a bit of theirs too.

They left the nightstand heading down the avenue towards the gardens, when it was almost dark at night.

It breathed well. There would be a full moon that night.

They walked for a few minutes in silence.

Next, Gretel chose a well-placed wooden bench in the corner.

"Let's sit down, Max. I love you, how easily one can make mistakes in relation to others. It is wonderful to be able to say: I love you.

Max felt intense heat in his chest.

Gretel even looked younger with that new light in her pupils.

To hell with everything! The war, Oslo, the Gestapo, the Russian spies ... Life is savored in sips, it is true, and it is the greatest stupidity in the world not to take advantage of one of those few sips, but that can fill a life.

"Wonderful» Gretel, "Max whispered.

They were alone on the bench, in that narrow garden. Max couldn't wait any longer. I needed Gretel, I needed her kiss ", I needed that sip of happiness.

He put both arms around her, greedily, - and looked into her eyes, gleaming. He recognized her;

Mysteriously, almost without intervening the will of both, their lips joined long, almost uneasily.

The next sip that life would provide could be bitter,

END